Heart O'Mine gave a short, sharp hough. Her tail began its warning dance on the floor. Tucking the dragon hatchling in the crook of his elbow and cradling it against his chest, Jakkin picked up the lamp with the other hand. "You have your nine, great mother," he said to the hen. "This *one* is mine. I shall make this one a great fighter. I swear it."

He slipped back into the hallway, hung the lamp up, and pushed the door shut with his shoulder. Then he went out into the night.

JANE YOLEN is the author of more than sixty books for children and young adults. *Dragon's Blood* is her first fantasy novel. A native of New York City, Ms. Yolen was graduated from Smith College and now lives with her husband and their three children in Hatfield, Massachusetts.

SARKKHAN'S NURSERY

SUKKER'S MARSH

COPSE OF SPIKKA TREES

Main road to Krakkow and Rokk →

Dikes

Dikes

SARKKHAN'S HOUSE

to Rokk 320 km.
to Krakkow 15 km.
to Krakkow-Minor Pit 27 km.

Narrakka River

DESERT

Dikes

FARMLAND

W   E
S

Oasis 5 km.

Dikes

CORRAL

STUD BARN

INCUBARN

HOSPICE

BONDHOUSE

Private dirt road

B.OTEL

dragon's blood

a fantasy by Jane yolen

LAUREL·LEAF BOOKS

LAUREL-LEAF BOOKS bring together under a single imprint outstanding works of fiction and nonfiction particularly suitable for young adult readers, both in and out of the classroom. Charles F. Reasoner, Professor Emeritus of Children's Literature and Reading, New York University, is consultant to this series.

Published by
Dell Publishing Co., Inc.
1 Dag Hammarskjold Plaza
New York, New York 10017

For information address
Delacorte Press, New York, New York.
Laurel-Leaf Library ® TM 766734,
Dell Publishing Co., Inc.

ISBN: 0-440-91802-2

RL: 7.3

Reprinted by arrangement with Delacorte Press
Printed in the United States of America
First Laurel-Leaf printing—March 1984

For Jeff, Joan, Jim, and Scott,
my first SF friends

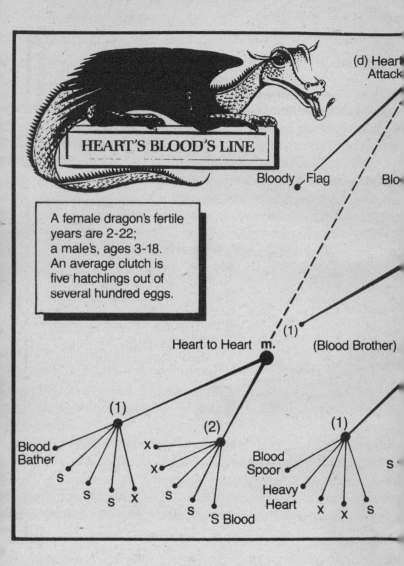

HEART'S BLOOD'S LINE

A female dragon's fertile years are 2-22; a male's, ages 3-18. An average clutch is five hatchlings out of several hundred eggs.

(d) Heart Attack

Bloody Flag

Blo

Heart to Heart m.

(1)

(Blood Brother)

(1)

Blood Bather

s

s s x

(2)

x

x

s

s

'S Blood

(1)

Blood Spoor

Heavy Heart

x x s

s

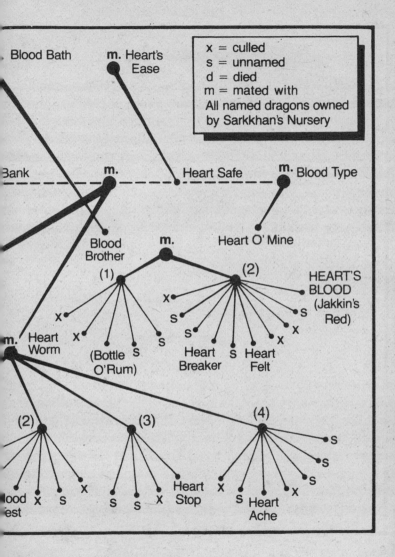

Blood Bath

m. Heart's Ease

x = culled
s = unnamed
d = died
m = mated with
All named dragons owned
by Sarkkhan's Nursery

Bank **m.** Heart Safe **m.** Blood Type

Blood Brother **m.** Heart O' Mine

(1) (2) HEART'S BLOOD (Jakkin's Red)

x s

x x s s x

m. Heart Worm

x s s

(Bottle O'Rum) s Heart Breaker s Heart Felt

(2) (3) (4) s

s

s

lood est x s x s s x Heart Stop x s Heart Ache x

Austar IV is the fourth planet of a seven-planet rim-system in the Erato Galaxy. Once a penal colony, marked KK29 on the convict map system, it is a semi-arid, metal-poor world with two moons.

Austar IV is covered by vast deserts, some of which are cut through by small, irregularly surfacing hot springs, and several small sections of fen lands. There are only five major rivers: the Narrakka, the Rokk, the Brokk-bend, the Kkar, and the Left Forkk.

Few plants grow on the deserts: some fruit cacti and sparse, long-trunked palm trees. The most populous plants are two wildflowering bushes called burn-wort and blisterweed. (See color section.)

There is a variety of insect and pseudo-lizard life, the latter ranging from small rock runners to elephant-sized dragons. (See article and holo sections, Vol. 6.) Unlike Earth *reptilia*, the Austarian dragon-lizards are warm-blooded, with pneumaticized bones for reduction of weight and a keeled sternum where the flight muscles are attached. They have membranous wings with jointed ribs that fold back along the animals' bodies when the dragons are earthbound. Stretched to the fullest, an adult dragon's wings are twice its body size. From claw to shoulder, some specimens have been measured at thirteen feet. These dragons were almost extinct when the planet was first settled by convicts and guards from Earth in 2303. But several generations later, the Austarians domesticated the few remaining dragons, selectively breeding them for meat and leather and the gaming arenas, or "pits."

The dragon pits of Austar IV were more than just the main entertainment for the early settlers. Over the years, the pits became central to the Austarian economy. Betting syndicates developed, and starship crews on long rim-world voyages began to frequent the planet for illicit gambling.

In 2485, under the control of Galaxian Law, illegal gamesters were transported from Austar IV to KK47, and a constitution spelling out the government's role in the economy—including control over the gambling—was voted in. A caste system of masters and bond slaves, the remnants of the convict-guard hierarchy, was established. And The Rokk, which had been the fortress center of the ruling guards and their families, was made into the capital city.

Now that the inhabitants of Austar IV are many generations removed from their convict ancestors, the planet is no longer off limits to long-haul starships, although the Erato Galaxy itself is still only in protectorate status. However, because of the fighting pit dragons, Austar has become one of the better known R&R planets in the explored universe.

excerpt from *The Encyclopedia Galaxia*,
29th edition, Vol. 1, AAAL–BASE

the
hatchling

1

The twin moons cast shadows like blood scores across the sand. Jakkin hunkered down in a bowl-shaped depression and listened. Inside the wood-and-stone Dragonry he could hear the mewling and scratching of hatchlings as they pipped out of their shells. One more night and the hatching would be complete. One more night and he could steal in and pick out a hatchling to raise in secret out in the sands.

As he listened, Jakkin stroked the leather bond bag that hung from his neck chain. The bag held only a few coins. But Jakkin knew that once he had trained his dragon to fight in the pits, his bag would be plump and jangling with gold. Then no one could call him bonder again, and he would answer to no master's call but his own. He would be a boy no longer, but a man.

The rustlings inside the nursery increased as more and more hatchlings caught Jakkin's scent. They began to squeak their distress, a high peeping that multiplied quickly. In the nearby stalls, the hen dragons stomped their feet. They were well used to the man-smell but the panic of the newborn nestlings made them restless. Their huge clawed feet beat out challenges to the intruder near the clutch. Any moment now, a hen might roar, and *that* would wake any sleeping bonder within hearing.

Jakkin did not dare stay longer, but what did that matter? He had heard the sound of the hatchlings and he knew how close the pipping was to being finished. As a lower stallboy, he was not allowed into the incubarns. His job was to clean the stud stalls and bathe the big male dragons: dust and fewmets, fewmets and dust. He was no better than a mecho garbage collector, but at least he did not clank like one, disturbing the great cock dragons in their stalls. Few of the male dragons could tolerate the sound and smell of a mechanical heapster without hackling, their collars of hardened neck flesh raising up for a fight. A hackled dragon was no good for stud. It took days to calm one down. So humans, bonders, had to serve as waste collectors even on the most modern worm farm.

Jakkin knew the stud barn well, but the incubarn he could only imagine from the sounds. Tomorrow night, when the hatching was complete, he would find his way into those half-lit, cozy compartments where the temperature was kept at a constant 34°C. He would find his way and get himself a snatchling, and begin the transformation of bond boy into master in one quick, secret, silent act.

Jakkin turned and ran, bent over, towards the northernmost corner of the building. He waded across the stone weir, knee-deep in the water that was channeled through the Dragonry from the Narrakka River. At the third join, he climbed out again, but kept low until he came to the dunes, another shadow in a night of shadows.

The desert air dried his legs quickly. The water had come nowhere near the bottoms of his thigh-length bonder pants. He checked the horizon for unfamiliar shapes, watchers in the night, and then stood up, but only for a moment. He took the whisker from the sheath on his belt and began to broom his footsteps away. It made the going slow, and his back ached with the effort, but he did not dare leave prints to show that anyone had gone out across the sands. Bonders, lacking most entertainments, loved to gossip. At night in the bondhouse, once the lights were out, there was little else to do until sleep claimed them.

Jakkin had a few hours before the cold of Dark-

After. He planned to use them to check again on the crops of blisterweed and burnwort he was growing in his hidden oasis. Everything had to be ready for the arrival of the snatchling. He dared leave nothing to chance.

Jakkin thought, and not for the first time, how his inability to sense anything in the egg made stealing a dragon so difficult. Eggs were never counted, hatchlings were. That was because so few of the eggs actually hatched. Anyone could steal an egg unnoticed. But unless the thief could sense the living dragon within the shell, his chances of success were small.

And Jakkin did not have that sense. His talent was with the grown dragons, like his father before him. But his father had never had any time to teach Jakkin training skills. He had died beneath the claws of a feral dragon he had tried to train out in the sands when Jakkin was very young. Jakkin's mother had buried her man and then sold Jakkin and herself into bond for food and shelter. She had died, mourning, within the month, leaving Jakkin with scant memories, half-remembered stories his mother had told him, and a bond bag he was much too small to fill.

He thought back on his past as he whisked away his footprints, but without bitterness. What was, was. Bonders said, "You can fill no bag with regrets." What mattered now was stealing an egg, an egg containing a live dragon, without being caught. Then he had to watch over it until it hatched, and train it in secret to be a proper fighter. A champion in the Pits—a big, bright, responding red with a terrible roar and flames six or seven meters long—could buy Jakkin out of bond. Such a dragon had not been seen on Austar IV for as many years as Jakkin could recall. But he was determined to find one, raise it up, train a champion, fill his bag, and become a master. And becoming a master, he would become a man.

Jakkin was so lost in his dreaming, he came to the oasis sooner than he expected. It was only wide enough for a wellspring and a crude reed shelter. He had found the stream by chance when wandering alone in the sands several years earlier on the anniversary of his father's death. Then he had not known enough to broom away his steps. Anyone could have followed him—and shared his find. He had been lucky that time, for his tracks had drifted back into the dunes, covered by the pervasive wind-dervishes that deviled this part of the planet.

The warm spring rose out of nowhere and disappeared as quickly, a bright ribbon of blue-white water running east to west a scant ten meters. It had no rocks or faults in the bed to make it bubble, and so it moved quietly the length of its run.

7

Yet it shimmered against the sand unexpectedly, like dragon scales in the sun. The western end was rimmed with sand-colored kkhan reeds.

When Jakkin had first found the spring, he had begun his digging with his hands. On subsequent trips he had brought a small shovel, borrowed from the Nursery supply room, and long since returned there. Slowly, and with much perseverance, he had widened the western edge to make a pool. The pool was large enough for a boy to swim in, though too shallow for deep dives. And for four years the oasis had been his secret place. He came when work was finished or on his Bond-Off, the semi-monthly holiday each bonder had from the Dragonry. Jakkin had told no one about it, not even Slakk or Errikkin, his two closest bondmates. They chose to spend their Bond-Offs with the others, stuffing themselves at the Krakkow Stews or gaming at its Minor Pit. As young bonders, they mostly watched at the Pit, having little in the way of coins with which to bet. Some of the older bond boys spent their time and gold at the Baggeries as well, where girls waited to be filled like empty bags. But Jakkin preferred the silent, simple pleasures of his oasis and the knowledge that the few coins in his bag were in no danger of being lessened by trips into town.

It was the wellspring that had helped him decide to steal an egg. It could provide shelter and the promise of provisions. And so Jakkin had spent every free moonrise and Bond-Off at the oasis, planting a small patch of blisterweed and burn-wort along the side of the spring, milking plants near Sukker's Marsh for the seeds. It had taken him the better part of the year to sow enough to provide an adequate crop for his worm.

Jakkin walked along the weed and wort patch. In the moonlight the plants sent up smoke ghosts, a healthy sign. He knew better than to touch the growing red stalks, for they could leave painful burns. Only when the plants stopped smoldering and leafed out could they be touched safely: milked for seeds, picked and crushed for dragon-food, or rolled for smokers like old Likkarn, who could not do without the weed.

Jakkin looked at the weed patch critically. He was pleased. There should be more than enough for his snatchling, especially since a dragon did not start eating until it had shed its eggskin, after three or four days. By then the plants would be ready, their pale red jagged-toothed leaves veined with the protein-rich sap that showed up a deep maroon in maturity.

Glancing quickly at the sky, Jakkin saw that the second moon, Akka, had already chased its older brother, Akkhan, across to the horizon. There they sat like giant eggs on the rim of the world. Soon they would seem to break apart, spilling a pale glow across the line where land and sky met, a cold false dawn. Once that happened, there would be four hours of Dark-After, those wretched hours when it was too cold for a human to stay out unsheltered in the sand. The reeds could house a hatchling, keeping its sun-sensitive eggskin shadowed in the daylight as easily as a hen dragon could. And once the dragon was fully scaled out, the sun could not harm it. But the reeds were useless at night. For dragons it did not matter. They did not mind the cold. But Jakkin knew he would have to hurry back, whisking away his returning tracks, before Dark-After settled its icy hold on the world.

2

Jakkin was into the deepest part of his sleep, dreaming of great eggs from which red curls of silent smoke rose, when the clanging of the breakfast bell woke him. Automatically he reached under his bed and with one arm dragged out his tunic and pants. Still lying down, eyes closed, he maneuvered into his clothes. Then he sat up on the side of his bed and thrust his feet into his sandals, oblivious of Slakk's legs hanging down from the upper bunk.

"Look out, worm waste," Slakk called and jumped, just missing Jakkin. "I almost landed on your head this time." He turned and punched Jakkin's bag companionably. "I swear, you're less awake than any bonder I know. What's the matter? Empty bag?" As if punctuating the question, he took another poke at Jakkin's bag, which clinked a quick answer. Dark, ferret-eyed Slakk bent down to tie his sandals, still talking in his insistent, whiny voice. "Less awake each day. Wonder what he's doing out half the night. Is it the Pits, I ask? He doesn't answer. The Stews? Will he respond? How about . . ." He stood, facing Jakkin again.

Jakkin grunted. Let Slakk think what he will. The image of the spirals of smoke signaling from the weed and wort patch filled his mind. Jakkin gave a second meaningless grunt and stood. He always found it hard to speak before he had gulped down his first cup of *takk*.

"Leave him alone, Slakk," called out the boy in the next bunk. "You know how he is in the morning." The boy leaped down from the bunk with an easy grace and put his hand out to Jakkin. "Never mind this talking lizard, silent one. I'll lead you straight to the *takk* pot. Then, perhaps, you will honor us with your words."

Jakkin refused Errikkin's hand but Errikkin was not insulted. He was never insulted. It was impossible to make him be anything but pleasant, a trait that annoyed Jakkin. He tied his sandals and then the three of them went towards the common room with Slakk in the middle holding a nonstop monologue about pit fighting. The monologue ended only when they were seated at their table.

There were twelve tables in all, and almost all

were filled. Jakkin, Slakk, and Errikkin sat with six other young bonders. There were three girls' tables. The rest of the tables were for the older bonders, most of whom, for one reason or another, had never been able to fill their bags with enough gold to buy their way out of bond. Only one table held both free men and women: those who were walking out together or pair-bonded, and Akkhina —little, lithe, black-haired Akki, who should have been at the Baggeries, Slakk said, but who preferred working around dragons and choosing her own men. Slakk always said that with a sly smile, as if there were more he could tell if he wanted, as if he had spent time with her. But Jakkin was sure it was all posture and bluff. Though Slakk was sixteen, Jakkin doubted he had ever been near a girl, any girl, not even a girl from the local Baggery.

The table was set with bowls, cups, and cutlery. Unlike some breeders, Master Sarkkhan had always supplied knives as well as forks and spoons to his bonders. They were well fed and well kept, and there was rarely a fight. In the center of each table stood the *takk* pot full of the rich, hot, wine-colored drink. The cook, old Kkarina, made it as thick as the mud of the stud baths; she claimed that if it were any thinner it lost much of its protein and all of its taste. Platters of lizard eggs, boiled in the shell, and heavy slabs of lizard meat sat next to the *takk* pot. The boys wasted little

13

time heaping their bowls. Jakkin was suddenly starving. He wondered if it was because of his late nights or his fears.

"I bet it's Bloody Flag and Blood Brother today," said Slakk, his mouth full of the juicy meat. "It's that time again. *Fewmets*, I hate that Brother. His is always the messiest stall, and besides, he loves to nip."

"I'll take him for you," said Jakkin. The first cup of *takk* had restored his tongue and burned courage through his body. "He never nips me."

"None of them ever nip *you*," said Errikkin pleasantly. "You've got something. Trainer blood. Like your dad. I bet even old Sarkkhan himself doesn't have your touch."

Jakkin looked down into his second cup of *takk* and stirred it slowly with a spoon. The deep red drink moved sluggishly. He knew that Errikkin was just being agreeable again, saying something to please, but it was something that Jakkin felt, too. Still he didn't dare voice it aloud. Bragging, like regrets, filled no bag.

"Will you take Brother to the bath, too?" Slakk never strayed far from his own concerns in any conversation. "His skin is getting flaky—the scales don't shine. We noticed it last time, Errikkin and me. And old Likkarn says . . ." Slakk spat expertly between his outspread second and third fingers, the sign of dragon horns. None of the boys liked

Likkarn, who was in charge of the bonders. He was too fussy and unforgiving, and quite brutal in his punishments. "Old Likkarn says *Scales like mud, little stud; scales like the sun, fine work done.* Old Likk-and-Spittle's full of such stuff."

Jakkin smiled into his cup.

"*Hush,*" Errikkin hissed. "He might hear you. Then where would we be?"

"Nowhere that's any worse than where we are now," replied Slakk.

Errikkin's concern was a formality. Likkarn was too many tables away to hear Slakk's complaints and Jakkin's replies or to register Errikkin's desperate hissing. He sat with the older bonders and the free men, the ones who really ran the Dragonry for the often absent Sarkkhan. They spent each morning meal working out the day's schedule, which Likkarn then scripted. Every bonder knew his or her own mark, and the mark of individual dragons, but beyond that few of them knew how to read. Or write. Likkarn, so the gossip ran, knew how to write because he had been born free. And he scripted each day's schedule with an elegant hand, though given the bonders' illiteracy, that was more ritual than anything else. Likkarn would read the day's worksheet out loud as the others filed out the door, and then hang the assignments on the wall. Even though he was a weeder, he was tolerated by Sarkkhan because he could read and script. Few of the bonders could read and fewer still could script. It was something taught only to free men and women.

The boys got up together. Errikkin was in the lead, Jakkin next. Several of the smaller boys slipped in between him and Slakk.

Slakk whispered at Jakkin's back, "Was I right? The schedule. Was I right?"

Jakkin checked the marks next to his name and Slakk's, reading them upside-down on the chart in front of Likkarn. Jakkin's mother had taught him to read early, before they had been in bond. He could still remember the chanting tone she adopted for drilling his letters. Jakkin had practiced faithfully to honor her memory. The few coins he ever spent went for books, which he kept hidden with his clothes under his bed. His ability to read, which he did not trouble to hide, was one of the things that Likkarn hated. The old weeder jealously guarded his right to script the schedule. He needn't have bothered. Jakkin could read—but he could not write.

Turning, Jakkin called lightly over the heads of the younger boys, "You were right, Slakk."

Likkarn scowled and read off Jakkin's duties anyway, his voice edged with anger. "*Jakkin: Bloody Flag and Blood Brother. Stalls and baths.* And be sure they're quieted down. If any of them hackle, you're in for it."

"Don't forget"—Slakk's whine began before they were out of the door—"you promised. You promised you'd take . . ."

Jakkin nodded and walked quickly to get away from Slakk's voice. He willed himself to remember the oasis and the sounds in the incubarns. He was halfway to the stud barn when Slakk caught up with him.

"You did promise, you know."

"Oh, lizard lumps, shut up already. I know I promised." Jakkin rarely got angry with anyone except Slakk. Then at his friend's crestfallen look, Jakkin was immediately contrite. "I'm sorry, Slakk. I didn't mean to yell. I'm just . . ." He stopped, horrified with himself. He had been about to confess to Slakk how tired he was and why.

Errikkin turned back and interrupted them. "It's just been too many days since your last Bond-Off," he supplied. He put his arm over Jakkin's shoulder. "That's all."

Jakkin nodded. They all accepted that explanation and went on to the barn.

The stud barn was twice as high as the bondhouse, to accommodate the size of the big male dragons. Inside on the south wall were individual stalls which simulated the pumice caves where mature males lived in the wild. Since the males paired off when it was not rutting season, leaving the hen dragons to raise the hatchlings, the studs had linked stalls throughout the barn. An un-paired stud often went into a decline and was not good for mating. The north wall stalls were used for the male pit fighters.

In the center of the barn was the great hall, where hen dragons in heat were brought to the studs. The hall was an arena-sized courtyard, without a roof, to accommodate the frantic, spiral-ing courting flights. It had a soft, mossy floor for the act itself.

Throughout the barn was a system of stone dikes that carried water in from, and out again to, the Narrakka River. It was triple-forked inside the building. One fork funneled drinking water into the individual stalls and a clear, flowing drinking stream into the mating hall. The second funneled out waste water that was used for cleaning the barn. The third fork ran directly into the baths, those tremendous pools of mud in which the drag-ons rolled and sank up to their eyes, to be cooled after mating or fights or twice a month in off-rut. The third fork also filled the cisterns in the shower room, with run-offs back into the outlying swamps.

The boys went into the barn, and the deep, cool, musky air assaulted them. Jakkin breathed deeply, and smiled. Dragon smells and dragons. It was really what he loved most in the world.

"Phew," said Slakk. "The first thing I am going to do when I buy out of bond is to celebrate the end of this smell. I'm never going to work with dragons again."

"What will you do, then?" asked Errikkin. "What else do you know?"

"I know food," Slakk answered. "I might apprentice to a cook. Or run a Baggery. *That* might be a job for a man. Anything but being a slave to a worm."

Jakkin shook his head and was just going to reply when an incredible roar filled the hallway. It began on a deep bass note and wound its way up and up, without hesitation, until it screamed out its defiance beyond human hearing.

"That's Blood Brother," Jakkin remarked. "He knows it's his turn."

"Just as long as he doesn't hackle," said Errikkin.

"All roar and no fight," sneered Slakk. "That's why he's here. After his first two wins, he refused to go into the pit again."

It was a cynical assessment of the great dragon's skill, but even Errikkin had to agree. Blood Brother's history was known even to the stallboys. Two tremendous fights with older, cunning dragons, and the next time the trainers had tried to lead Brother into the Nursery truck to drive to a Pit, he had simply collapsed at the barn door. A ton of fighting dragon lying on the ground was not something that could be moved easily. Likkarn had tried the prod-sticks and even a shot with the stinger, set below Stun. But Brother would not move until the truck had driven off without him. Only then had he stood and moved placidly back inside the barn on his own.

"But he's a fantastic stud," Jakkin reminded them. "His hatchlings have won in pits all over the world."

Slakk shrugged and Errikkin smiled. Then the three of them padded down the hall to the dragon stalls.

3

Blood Brother turned his great black shrouds of eyes towards the boys, but in the neighboring stall Bloody Flag continued to munch mindlessly on blisterwort. Brother showed his annoyance by shifting his weight back and forth and houghing.

Jakkin ran his fingers through his hair, then touched the dimple on his cheek that was as deep as a blood score. He always did that when he was nervous, and though he never would have let Slakk and Errikkin know it, Blood Brother was the one dragon he did not wholly trust. Brother was so unpredictable—one minute almost thrumming, that deep-throated purr that a contented dragon used, the next sending warning straggles of smoke through his slits. Still, it did not do to let a dragon know how nervous you were. Some bonders claimed dragons could smell fear on you. Jakkin supposed that was how his father had been killed by the feral in the sands. Besides—all dragons, he reminded himself with the conventional trainer's wisdom, all dragons are feral, even though they have been domesticated for over two centuries. And especially dragons like Blood Brother.

As if hearing his name, Brother jerked his head up. Deep inside the black eyes there was an iridescent flicker, the sign of a fighter. Involuntarily Slakk stepped back. Errikkin stood his ground. Only Jakkin went forward, holding out a hand.

"Hush, hush, beauty," he crooned, letting Brother sniff his hand. "It's the baths for you."

Jakkin kept up the soothing babble until the head of the beast started to weave back and forth and the boys could feel the thrumm of content humming along the floor. Errikkin unlatched the stall gate and Jakkin reached up, hooked his finger around the dragon's ear, and backed him out of the stall.

As Jakkin led the dragon down the hall, Slakk ran ahead to the bell pull which signaled throughout the other halls that a dragon was unstalled. No one wanted to be in the way of those great back feet or foreshortened front feet with claws as hard and yellow as old bone. On hearing the bell, anyone in the barn would press in against the evenly spaced hallway niches until the dragon had gone by. Only the trainer, leading the dragon by ear or halter, pacing by its side, could be reasonably assured of safety, but even a good trainer could be accidentally clawed. Old Likkarn had a dozen scars punctuating the long, stringy sentences of veins that ran down his legs. And the rumor was that Sarkkhan himself looked like the map of Austar, pocked and pitted from his years with dragons. But that Jakkin knew only from gossip. He had never been up close to Master Sarkkhan. For all Jakkin knew, the man's body might be as smooth as a Baggery girl's, though that was highly unlikely. Anyone who worked around dragons for long wore blood wounds.

Jakkin clucked with his tongue to let the dragon know he was still there. "Just be a good fellow," Jakkin sang to Brother as they went along the hall. It was early, and no one was in the niches; there was nothing to distract them as they went down to the baths. Jakkin knew that Slakk and Errikkin would use this time to clean the stall, raking out the old fewmets, patting down the dust, settling new straw for bedding. They would crush fresh wort and weed in the feed box and maybe, with extra time, polish Brother's nameplate. Sarkkhan was rich enough to afford metal ones.

Each dragon had a bath once every other week, but the stalls had to be cleaned every other day. Dust and fewmets, fewmets and dust. That was usually a stallboy's life. So Jakkin welcomed the chance to be more than a human pit cleaner, and he loved to take the dragons to their baths.

Blood Brother, smelling the mud, threw his head up; Jakkin lost his hold on the dragon's ear. "Worm bag," Jakkin muttered under his breath as the dragon reared up slightly, fanning the close air with his front feet. There was not enough room for Brother to complete a hind leg stand, but Jakkin could feel the air currents change as the dragon lashed his tail from side to side. The thump-thumping as the tail hit the solid wooden walls was echoed in Jakkin's chest. He would have to get Brother quickly into the baths and quieted down before the dragon did damage to the building or to himself. Either way and old Likkarn would have Jakkin back spreading fewmets on the weed and wort patches for a month. It wasn't bad work, but he preferred dragons.

Jakkin plunged between Brother's front feet and lunged for the bath door. It was a dangerous move, but unpredictable enough to shock the dragon into backing up a pace. Jakkin lifted the latch and rode the doorstep platform in and over the sunken bath room.

Blood Brother crowded in behind and plunged into the deep mudhole. It cooled his temper at once and he began to splash and snuffle in the bath like a hatchling.

From his perch on the swinging platform Jakkin smiled. All of the dragon's ferocity seemed to slip away, and what was left was a rather silly, over-sized lizard, burbling and rolling about in a pool of muck.

"And what was I scared of?" Jakkin said to Brother, but the dragon ignored him completely.

Jakkin took a large wire brush from its hook on the door and sat down on the step, his legs hanging over the side. His perch swayed back and forth. He knew that in a little while the dragon would have had enough of plunging around in the mud and would want his scales scrubbed. Dragons in the wild groomed one another with teeth and claws and a tongue as rough as bristles. But domesticated dragons, though paired in stalls, were not let loose in the baths together. Their play was too rough for even the strongest wood and stone building. Besides, most dragons got so they preferred the wire brush, which could reach the most incredibly delightful places when wielded by a sensitive human groom.

Blood Brother sank down to the bottom of the mud bath. Only his eyes, now shuttered with their membranous second lid, showed above the brown sludge. His ears twitched constantly. After a minute, even the ears stopped moving and Blood Brother slept.

"Pleasant dreams," mumbled Jakkin. He knew

25

that the dragon—and not the human—would choose the time of grooming. Then, though he tried not to, he dozed off as well.

Jakkin had no idea how long they had slept. One moment he was dreaming of the oasis, clean and bright and shimmering in the desert sun, and the next he was awakened by a playful, muddy nudge from Blood Brother's nose. It was forceful enough to have knocked him from his perch if the door hadn't swung towards the far wall.

Jakkin grabbed the metal chain attached to the wall and leaped onto the catwalk. He pushed the door back with one foot and watched it lock shut with a satisfying click. His heart was racing. Falling asleep on the door was a stupid thing to have done, especially with Blood Brother in the bath. If he had fallen into that deep mud with the dragon, there would have been little chance of his escaping. Recently, one bonder in a nursery on the far side of Krakkow had died that way. It could not have been a pleasant death.

"Come on, worm," he said aloud, amazed that his voice was not shaking. He held the brush behind him as he walked along the catwalk towards the shower room. The dragon followed, heaving himself out of the mud and onto the ramp with a loud sucking sound.

In the shower room, Jakkin stripped off his tunic and sandals but left his shorts on. And his bag. No bonder was allowed to remove the bag until it was full. Jakkin reached up and pulled the cord that started the shower. Brother was so becalmed from the mudbath, Jakkin no longer feared him.

The water began raining down on them and Jakkin moved around the great beast, heedless now of its claws. He scratched and polished the muddy scales. First the mud came off, then the patina of stall dust. Beneath were orange-red scales that shimmered in the flickering light of the shower room.

"Pretty, pretty," Jakkin crooned.

Blood Brother was not a deep wine red, which was the best color for a fighting dragon (for somehow color and ferocity were gene-linked). But his color was strong, and his scales, when clean, had the sheen and polish of hundreds of small rainbow mirrors. They were not spotty or off-color as some dragon scales were.

As he worked, Jakkin smiled and even whistled through his teeth. He was enjoying the cleaning as much as the dragon.

Blood Brother languorously stretched out his wings. Unfurled, they nearly touched the opposite walls. His wingspread was the widest in the Nursery, and it seemed to Jakkin that Brother enjoyed showing them off. When not confined in his stall, the dragon took every opportunity to stretch his magnificent wings.

Jakkin took a soft cloth from a hook and rubbed

the silky-tough membranes that stretched between the rock-hard wing ribs. He was especially
careful of the skin next to the right secondary,
where a series of four puckered scars bore witness
to Brother's time in the Pits.

Brother began to flinch as the cloth came close
to the scars, and Jakkin held on firmly to the wing.
"I'll be careful, fellow. You can't tell me that still
hurts after all this time. But I'll be careful." He
thought to himself that he'd have to be a fool *not*
to be careful. Brother had knocked one of the
older bonders senseless a year ago, smashing him
up against the shower wall, just for bearing down
too hard on that wing.

Hanging the cloth back on the hook, Jakkin
took up the brush again. He stood on tiptoe and
leaned against the dragon, clicking to it with his
tongue. Jakkin tried, as always, to reach Brother's
mind with his. Trainers were often able to have a
tenuous kind of mental bond with their worms. All
Jakkin could ever sense with Brother was a dark,
sluggish brooding, the color of bloody mud.

Jakkin clicked again and pushed Brother with
his shoulder. Slowly the dragon turned its head to
look at him and Jakkin tapped as far up Brother's
back as he could reach with the brush. With a
sigh, the worm lay down, first folding his short,
powerful forelegs, then squatting down on the
hind. Jakkin scratched the upper scales with a

gentle persistence. He worked his way down the slope of the neck, leaving the head for last.

Jakkin sat down in front of Brother and cradled the dragon's head in his lap. He began to croon a silly little song that had been sung in the bondhouse that month, a kind of dragon lullaby.

> Little flame mouths,
> Cool your tongues,
> Dreaming starts soon,
> Furnace lungs.
>
> Rest your wings now,
> Little flappers,
> Cave mouth calls
> To dragon nappers.
>
> Night is coming;
> Bank your fire,
> Time for dragons
> To retire.
>
> Hiss. Hush. Sleep.

As he sang, Jakkin brushed Brother's ears and around his horns, over the nose and under the chin. The beast began thrumming again in the same rhythm as the song. Then, as if to thank Jakkin for the grooming, Brother tried to groom in return, holding the boy down with one foreclaw and giving him long tongue swipes along the leg. The treatment was so rough and painful, Jakkin stopped singing and began to shout.

"Cut it out, you worm pile!" He banged Brother on the nose several times with the wire brush.

With a loud, rumbled hough, the dragon let him up.

Jakkin turned off the shower, grabbed up his clothes, and put them on hastily. Then he took Brother's ear and jerked him up. Forgetting the warning bell pull because of the pain in his leg, and limping, Jakkin led Blood Brother back around to his newly cleaned stall. Luckily no one was in the hall.

Slakk and Errikkin were sitting by the stallside. Slakk was fingering his bag and talking. Errikkin was smiling and nodding his head. They jumped up when they saw the dragon coming.

"Fewmets!" Slakk yelled. "Why didn't you warn us? That big lump could have stepped on us and then where would we be?"

Jakkin didn't reply but shoved the dragon into the stall. Smelling the fresh food, Brother went in willingly. Jakkin latched the door and turned back to his friends.

It was Errikkin who noticed his leg. "That's awful red. You look like you've lost some skin. Does it hurt?" he asked, pointing, his bland-handsome face creased with worry.

Before Jakkin could answer, Slakk said, "I *told* you he was dangerous. They ought to send him to the Stews before he kills someone."

Jakkin answered angrily. "He was just being playful. And grateful. And—worm waste!"

"What is it?" asked Errikkin, parading his concern.

"I left the bagged brush in the shower."

"I'll get it!" cried Slakk, jumping up. Before Jakkin could stop him, Slakk was running down the hall, his bag bouncing crazily against his tunic. But once around the turning, he slowed down. He would walk from here. If he took enough time, the others would start on the next stall and bath without him.

4

At the shower room door, Slakk hesitated, bent down, and removed his sandals. Wet feet would dry faster than wet shoes. He heard a noise and looked up. Likkarn was standing over him, glowering, the bath brush in his hand.

"I . . . it . . . wasn't me," Slakk began under the man's hooded gaze.

"It *will* be when I get through with you, you empty-bagged piece of waste. Tossing Master Sarkkhan's property around and dodging work. I know you—bonder." Likkarn spoke it all with a quiet that exaggerated his fury, and his weed-reddened eyes seem to grow bloodier with each word. He grabbed up Slakk's tunic and slowly raised the boy off the floor so that only his toes touched.

Then he gave Slakk three hard shakes and dropped him. Slakk fell heavily, twisting his leg and giving a sharp cry of pain.

"Now, if it isn't you, who is it?" Likkarn asked. He knew that fear and pain could control the bond boys and he used his knowledge with precision. In his blister fury, Likkarn was—like all weeders—practically unrestrainable. But during the day he did not allow himself to smoke. "Who —is—it?" he asked again, coldly, spacing the words without obvious passion—that he saved for the dragons he helped train and for his nights of blisterweed.

Again Slakk sobbed out, "It wasn't me." And then, under his breath, as if whispering might excuse his betrayal, he added, "It was Jakkin. Not me. Jakkin."

Likkarn stepped over him and went down the hallway, heedless of Slakk's sobbing. He strode eagerly, not bothering to mask his elation. Jakkin was the one boy who irritated him beyond measure; Jakkin, with his sure touch with dragons, his aloofness, his ability to read. Jakkin had already caught Sarkkhan's eye. The Nursery owner had asked about Jakkin once or twice already. Such a boy, a hard worker who kept himself apart from the other bonders in their games, could not be easily manipulated. "It will be a pleasure breaking Jakkin over *this*," Likkarn told himself, knowing it would keep the other bonders in line, knowing that to empty the boy's bag over such a slight infraction would be personally sweeter than waiting for an important mistake. He allowed himself a small smile.

Errikkin was already in Bloody Flag's stall, calming the dragon in preparation for the bath. Flag was a phlegmatic beast, hard to rouse even for mating. That calmness was what Sarkkhan hoped to breed into future dragons, without Flag's habitual torpor. Breeding was an inexact science, but Sarkkhan's work had always had a high percentage of correct guesses.

Jakkin was still with Blood Brother, finishing the grooming by trimming the dragon's nails with a large hasp. It was a job that had to be done within the confines of the stall so that the dragons could not strike out if a sensitive claw was cut carelessly. Many breeders had their stud dragons declawed, since the beasts were no longer used in the Pits. But according to Sarkkhan, a declawed dragon could not catch its mate easily in flight and the extra energy the stud had to expand chasing down the elusive female reduced its potency.

Jakkin did not know if such a thing was true, but still, he thought, "If Flag were declawed he'd *never* breed. Not if it meant an extra long chase." He must have said it out loud, because there was an answering chuckle from Errikkin in Flag's stall.

34

Neither boy heard Likkarn coming down the hall. The old trainer moved silently over to Blood Brother's stall, his fury and eagerness tight behind his smile. The dragons sensed Likkarn's height-ened emotions. Flag merely houghed once and stopped. But Brother began to sway back and forth.

Jakkin stood, not knowing what was wrong. He tried to calm the worm, stroking its nose and crooning to it. But the dragon would not be soothed. Trails of smoke began to leak through his slits. Jakkin closed his eyes and again tried to reach the dragon's mind, but the dark red mud it projected was now shot through with flashes of bright yellow lightning. Brother was really dis-turbed. Jakkin knew that the only thing to do now was to get out of the stall as quickly as possible and bar the door. Then he would have to get one of the extinguishers—the stun guns—that hung by the main door. If necessary, he'd have to use the stinger to knock Brother out for a while. Once a dragon began thrashing, no one was safe.

Jakkin ducked under Brother's neck and slid along his side, timing his run to coincide with the sway. Just as Jakkin reached the door, Brother grunted and threw his head up, giving a soft whine. It was like the early screams of pit dragons warming to a fight. Jakkin knew that in minutes the dragon would hackle if he couldn't be put to sleep.

Jakkin clawed at the inside latch and pushed the door open. He started out and ran straight into Likkarn, who waited there.

"Messy," sneered the old bonder. "Careless and messy." He held up the bath brush like a weapon, and was so intent on beating the boy, he did not notice the dragon's whine.

"Blood Brother . . ." began Jakkin, trying to warn the trainer out of the stall doorway.

But Likkarn lifted the brush high up over his head and brought it down with contained fury on Jakkin's shoulder. The bristles made a bloody pattern where they slipped off Jakkin's tunic and onto skin. Jakkin cried out.

The dragon answered him, scream for scream, rearing up in a hind foot stand that pulled its leather halter out of the ring. As Brother's head touched the wooden ceiling beams, he dropped again, angered and confused, an orange light pinpointed in his black eyes. He kicked out with his rear legs, sending Jakkin tumbling into Likkarn. They fell together, the boy on top.

Blood Brother backed out of the stall screaming, and stepped slantwise on part of Jakkin's back, pressing the boy down heavily on the trainer. The dragon never noticed, but moved on, unfurling his wings until the tips touched the walls. The scarred wing scraped past a pair of hooks, and one hook caught the tender membrane, ripping it open. Frantically the dragon tried to shake his wing loose, screaming his fury over and over into the cavernous barn. Other dragons in their stalls up and down the hallway screamed back, terrifying the bonders working there. Errikkin cowered in Flag's stall, his back against the bin.

Blood Brother gave one last mighty pull and his wing tore free, the hot blood dripping down onto the dust, burning the floor boards where it fell. Three drops spattered onto Jakkin's back, leaving deep pits. But he had been unconscious since the first blow and did not feel the burns.

The dragon roared once, then stopped at the smell of his own blood and stood trembling.

Likkarn crawled out from under the boy's body and put his back against the wall. He edged towards the barn door where the extinguishers hung, three on a side. He moved slowly because he could feel that some of his ribs were broken and because he knew that any other sudden movement could send the dragon into new furies. Likkarn was breathing in great gasps by the time he reached the door. His fingers found the gun but his eyes never left the dragon. Trembling, he brought the stinger up and sighted between Brother's eyes, sliding the force regulator to Stun.

At the gun's movement, Brother moved his head up and whined once. Then he lowered it again and stared at Likkarn with shrouded eyes. He sensed, in a muddled way, the man's purpose. He whined again.

Likkarn's hand on the regulator hesitated, then rammed it right on to Kill. He fired once into the dragon's head, shattering the black eyes, and once more into the front of the neck, severing the sternum muscles and making a crimson flower burst and trickle down onto the dragon's breast. First the mighty wings collapsed helpless at the dragon's sides. Then slowly the great beast fell, shaking the floor of the barn. At his collapse, all the dragons in the stud barn set up a howling.

Tears, nowhere near as red as dragon's blood but colored from blisterweed, ran slowly down Likkarn's cheeks in familiar grooves.

"You gutless lizard," he hissed. "You piece of waste. Whine at me, will you? I bet everything I had on your third fight. You were going to be a champion. I was going to be a man once more. You ruined me."

Likkarn dropped the gun and walked over and began kicking the dying beast in the side. The rhythm of the blows seemed to echo in the hall. Kick after kick he delivered until the kicking tired him out. He began to tremble violently, the first sign of weed hunger or shock. He turned abruptly and went out of the barn, dropping the extinguisher in the doorway. He spoke to the first bonder he saw.

"Send Brother's carcass to the Stews. And get a good price for it. It's prime. Then take care of that other piece of waste, that boy Jakkin. *If* he's still alive."

Shaking off any help, and holding his sides, Likkarn went towards the bondhouse without looking back.

5

Jakkin waded through muddy nightmares and woke a dozen times. Each time pain and drugs sent him spiraling back to the blood-colored swamps where he slogged towards the light yet one more time.

At last he came to and discovered he was staring into a starched white pillowcase and breathing through it with difficulty. Since his bunk in the bondhouse did not include such niceties, he realized groggily that he must be in the hospice. He tried to turn over, and the pain in his shoulders and down his back was so intense, he screamed weakly and buried his face in the pillow again.

"I think you'll live," came an amused voice, cool and gentle.

Jakkin lifted his head and turned slowly till he reached the outer edge of the pain. He could see the speaker now. It was Akki, the girl that Slakk said should be in the Baggeries. Even in his state, Jakkin could see why. Her black hair hung straight down her back; her skin was the pale cream of a hatchling. She had a generous, mobile mouth that right now was laughing at him. Jakkin winced again and Akki moved to the head of the bed, where he could see her more easily. She held out a glass filled with iced *takk*.

"Here. Drink this. And now that we both know you'll make it, I have to get back to work. There are a couple of really sick people in here, you know. Not just ones with dragon footprints up and down their spines."

Jakkin groaned and managed to gasp out, "So that's what hurts." He had only a vague memory of what had happened, ending with Brother's kick.

"That and three nice deep blood scores," said Akki cheerfully. Her smile was slightly crooked. Jakkin liked that, except it made her seem to be enjoying his discomfort. "Too bad. They were the only pits on an otherwise scoreless body."

He could feel himself blushing and pushed the *takk* glass back into her hand. Then he buried his face in the pillow. When he raised his head again, Akki was gone. He couldn't decide if he was happy about her disappearance.

Jakkin glanced out of the window. It was shut

and the blackness outside made him gasp. It was almost Dark-After. Hurt or not, he would have to get out of the bed, out of the hospice, and back to the incubarn. The hatching must be nearly complete by now. If he didn't get himself an egg or a newborn hatchling before the morning count, it might be another year before he could try again.

He eased himself into a sitting position, keeping his mouth open. He breathed deeply, willing himself to forget the pulsing ache in his back, the three hotpoints of searing agony that were the blood scores. He put his feet over the side of the bed and waited out the next pulse of pain. Except for some bandages on his back, and his bond bag, he was naked. His pants and tunic were folded neatly on a chair by the bed. He managed to move to them, hunching like an old man, shuffling carefully so as not to jar his wounds.

"Fewmets," he cursed. "At this rate I'll be lucky to get out of *here* by dawn."

Somehow he managed to get into his pants. He had to carry his sandals and tunic. Inching towards the door, he listened for footsteps in the hallway. He heard none, opened the door, and sighed with relief to see that his room was only about ten meters from the front door. To call it walking, he thought, was an overstatement. He moved like an injured Fifty-Foot, the awkward insect that went in circles if it lost even a single leg. Only his back was not going to regenerate as quickly as a Fifty-Foot's foot. He was going to have this pain for a long time—and the blood scores forever.

By the glass door he hesitated once again. Pushing it open was going to require some extra effort. He saw that it was not quite Dark-After, but the two moons were squatting on the horizon and Akkhan was already leaking its color along the line. All the pain, his awkward, hurting shuffle, had been for nothing. He pounded his fist impotently on the door, almost hoping the glass would break. As he did so, he thought he felt something break open on his back. The new pain made him whimper and he slowly slid down the glass door and collapsed onto the floor.

Jakkin woke with his face in the pillow again and wondered if he had dreamed his walk down the hall.

"And what were you trying to do, hero?" Akki's amused voice told him it had not been a dream after all. "You managed to rip off a bandage and start some bleeding again. And I'm the only one on night duty. Do you know how heavy you are?"

Jakkin lifted his head high enough to see Akki scripting something on a chart at the foot of his bed. He noticed that his pants and tunic were once again on the chair and his embarrassment was so great he did not even blush this time, just put his head back on the pillow and was silent.

As if she had not noticed any movement, Akki continued her monologue. "Were you planning to run around in Dark-After? Hobble-hop here and there? Why, boy, enjoy your rest. You'll be back with the dragons soon enough. You remind me of . . . Why, even old Likk-and-Spittle let his broken ribs get him off for three days. He just lay here and loved every minute of our coddling. Loved it, that is, until Sarkkhan came here with blood on his mind and broke that bagged weeder back down to stallboy again. Imagine, extinguishing a stud like Blood Brother when all he had to do was stun the worm. All he had to do was . . ."

Jakkin pushed himself over on his side, ignoring the dancing knives in his back. "Three days? Likkarn was here three days? I don't understand. It's Dark-After. How could it be three days? *How long have I been here?*"

Akki came around with another glass of *takk*, this one steaming hot. She held it out to him. Her mouth was serious. "You've been in and out of consciousness almost a week," she said. "There was even a time when we thought we might lose you. But Sarkkhan said you have too much fight in you to die young, and that your head is harder than dragon bone. He should know. He has a head like that himself."

"A week. Dark-After a week!" Jakkin's face lost what color it had and he pushed Akki's hand away. The glass fell and splintered on the floor.

44

The *takk* splattered. Jakkin threw himself down on the pillow and began to weep, heedless of Akki's hands on his hair or her soothing voice. He was fifteen and could not remember ever crying before, not as a child when his father had died so brutally; not in bond when his mother slipped away so quietly in her sleep; not when Likkarn had tormented him with the memory of his father's death under the feral's claws. He sobbed— for this lost chance, for the death of Blood Brother, for the aching scores on his back, and even with the remembered pain of his parents' loss.

Akki's voice came to him as if from far away. "It's the medicine, Jakkin. The medicine makes you weak, makes you cry."

He ignored her and let the waves of uncontrollable sorrow wash over him until he fell into a deep, troubled sleep. When he woke again, it was afternoon and Akki was gone.

Getting out of bed and dressing was nowhere near as hard as it had been the day before. Jakkin's back was stiff and he had a continuing headache, but the dizziness, the depression, the pinpoints of pain were gone. He decided not to wait for a visit from the doctor. He had to find out what had happened in the week missing from his life. He had to know if all the hatchlings had already been counted and settled in with their hens.

The sun was bright and hot overhead, and there

45

was no breeze as Jakkin walked the short distance between the hospice and the barns. He met no one on the path. In the intense heat of the day, everyone either worked inside the cool barns or napped. Bonders worked.

Jakkin tried to remember back before he had been a bonder. He picked through his meager store of memories: the sight of his father bleeding on the sands while the feral dragon, a black blot in the sky, winged towards the farthest mountains; his mother threading her thin, fragile fingers through his as they walked towards Sarkkhan's Nursery, a pack filled with their few possessions on her back. Her voice came suddenly to him out of the past. "We may be bonders, but we will fill our bags ourselves." The memory of her voice was more vivid to him than the picture of his father's body. But whether that walk had occurred before they had become bonders or after, he did not know.

"I will fill my bag myself," he murmured, stroking the leather bag with two fingers.

When he entered the barn, the rush of cool air revived him. He wandered around the stalls, pausing for a minute at the empty one that had housed Blood Brother. He wondered whom they would pair with Flag now and if the dragon suffered from the loss of his companion. From the sounds of dedicated chewing coming from Flag's stall, it was hard to believe he had even noticed Brother was gone.

"I should have checked the work list," Jakkin thought, seeing neither Slakk nor Errikkin. Then, hearing a complaining voice from farther down the hall, he followed it to the stalls where Blood Spoor and Blood Bather, a pair of red-gold four-year-olds, were housed.

Slakk's voice came from Bather's stall. Jakkin climbed up carefully, winced, and looked over. Both Slakk and Errikkin were on their knees, trimming the dragon's nails.

"These nails are butter-soft," Slakk was saying. "Look, the hasp leaves grooves. I don't want to be blamed for ruining him."

"No one will blame you, Slakk," said Errikkin. "And I'll back you up."

"What's the use of trimming them anyway?" Slakk continued. "This one isn't going to be any good in the pit with those nails. Or for catching a female either. Why do you suppose Sarkkhan keeps him?"

Errikkin shrugged.

"I think he should go to the Stews," Slakk finished.

"You think they *all* should go to the Stews," Jakkin said from his perch. "Maybe it's a *re*-trait and not a *dom*. Maybe the soft nails won't be passed on. Trust Master Sarkkhan to know."

47

"Jakkin!" both boys cried. Errikkin stood up immediately and smiled, but Slakk was suddenly very busy with the hasp again.

"Don't worry, Slakk," Jakkin added. "I don't blame you for anything. I can fill my bag myself."

Slakk looked up, but his small-eyed face was wiped free of expression. He put his hand over his bag, completely covering it. "What should you blame me for?" he asked.

Errikkin stepped between them, reached up, and touched Jakkin's hand. "We've missed you," he said. "Slakk especially. He's had to do twice as much work as before. Or so he says."

Gingerly Jakkin climbed down from the fence and walked to the stall door. Errikkin lifted the latch and came out, shutting the door behind him. Slakk remained inside, ostensibly trimming the rest of the dragon's nails.

"I seem to have missed a lot," Jakkin said slowly.

Errikkin, sensing an opportunity to please, filled him in. His tendency was to elaborate on the accident and the killing of Blood Brother. Not wanting to make Errikkin suspicious, Jakkin did not hurry him through the story. So he heard twice about the shots that had destroyed the beast and how Likkarn had sworn that, in his haste and fear, he had mistakenly pushed the regulator past Stun to Kill.

"Even though you have to push extra hard to change the setting," Errikkin added. Then he acted out Sarkkhan's reaction when he found the old trainer smoking blisterweed in the bondhouse.

"Sarkkhan said, 'You've always hated that dragon, Likkarn.'" Errikkin tried to lower his voice as deep as the nursery owner's. "'You bet your bag on him and lost and you hated him for it.' 'No, Master Sarkkhan, I *loved* that worm. Raised him from a hatchling myself, I did,' Likkarn said as the smoke trickled out of his mouth." Errikkin put his hand over his bag in imitation.

"And what did Master Sarkkhan say to that?" Jakkin asked.

"He said . . ."

Errikkin was interrupted by Slakk, who came out of the stall now that the story was past his part in it. "He said, 'How many chances can I give you, Likkarn? We've known each other a long time. We were boys together. But how long can I trust a weeder?'"

"And then Likkarn said . . ." Errikkin tried to add.

"No, then Likkarn began to go into fury and jumped off his bunk screaming *There's no difference between us but half a bag!* And he ripped off his bag, which really *was* half full, and threw it into Sarkkhan's face. And then he followed the bag and leaped at Master Sarkkhan and started hitting him." Slakk finished the story so quickly he was out of breath.

Jakkin shook his head. "Crazy. Weeders are crazy. Even in blister fury Likkarn's no match for Master Sarkkhan. Sarkkhan must have killed him."

"No, that's the funny part," said Errikkin. "He only held the old man's arms until the fury wore itself out. Then he pushed Likkarn back on the bed and with tears in his eyes said, 'I'm sorry, Likkarn. Sorry for all we've meant to one another. Sorry for all the years we shared. But for the sake of the others, for the sake of Blood Brother, I'm going to have to break you. It's back to stallboy.' And he emptied Likkarn's bag into his hand, pocketed all the gold but the grave coin, and put the empty bag gently on the bed beside him."

Slakk nodded. "That's true. And we know because Akki was there and the doctor. And the doctor told Kkarina and she told . . ."

"Akki?" Jakkin looked puzzled. "What was she doing in the men's quarters? In Likkarn's room?"

Slakk smiled slyly. "She gets around. Around a lot. She was with the doctor and Sarkkhan when they went looking for Likkarn. Someone said he had been injured and they had already dealt with you."

"And I overheard some of it when I went to visit you in the hospice," Errikkin said.

"I don't remember you there."

Errikkin laughed and put his arm over Jakkin's shoulder. Jakkin winced at the weight and Errikkin pulled away. "You were out of it. For days and days. They finally made us get back to work and leave you alone."

"Not alone," suggested Slakk slyly. "I understand Akki stayed there all night."

"Yes, all night," Jakkin said fiercely, but he added, "I was out of it, as you said. And besides, she was just being a nurse."

The boys looked down at the ground as if a gulf had suddenly opened between them. Then Jakkin asked brightly, "Well, what else happened?"

"That's it," Slakk replied, turning and going back into the stall. "Are you going to help us finish?"

Errikkin pushed Jakkin away. "You look too white and shaky. Go on and rest. Slakk and I will finish up without you. After all, it isn't as if we had been expecting you to work today."

Suddenly Jakkin's head began to hurt again. He moved his shoulders up and down to test them. Pain shot tendrils along his spine. "Maybe I *will* go and lie down. Just today." He turned to go. Then, with as much offhandedness as he could muster, he asked, "How did the hatching go?"

Errikkin held up his hand in the wide-fingered greeting that meant everything was fine.

Slakk's voice floated back over the fence in a whine. "Come on, lizard lump, give me a hand."

Errikkin shrugged and gave a slight smile. "It

went fine. Supposed to have been the best hatching in years. See you at dinner."

Jakkin nodded and left. He didn't dare ask any more. That would seem suspicious. He would, indeed, have to fill his bag himself.

6

Making his way back to the bondhouse, Jakkin was suddenly aware of being hungry. He certainly couldn't fall asleep with his stomach making enough noise to wake the entire nursery. Perhaps Kkarina would let him have something to take back to his bed. She was a funny one, old Kkarina, sometimes easygoing and other times dangerous as a hen dragon after hatching. He would have to go about it carefully. He stroked his bag with one finger as he thought about the best way to approach her.

The door to the kitchen was open, sending out moist, fragrant smells. Jakkin had never been inside. It was a place of familiar mysteries. He stuck his head in tentatively, then let out an involuntary sigh.

Kkarina, standing over a great black pot, looked up. She smiled. "Come on in, come in. I can tell a hungry boy a mile away. Sit down and be my taster. From what I hear, that's about all the work you'll be managing for a few days."

Jakkin grinned wryly. So much for his careful approach. He sat down on a stool by the stove and waited.

Kkarina was a short, dark woman, with shoulders as broad as a man's and a waist that spoke of years of tasting in the kitchen. She wore only a thin short-sleeved jumper under a leather apron, and there were large gray stains under each arm. When she served the food, her neck and arms were always covered with a shapeless jacket. Jakkin was fascinated by her bare arms. They were vast but not fleshy. She radiated a kind of amused power. Jakkin wasn't actually afraid of her, but he would never want to get her angry. He opened his mouth and tried not to wince as she popped a spoon of pulpy mash into his mouth.

"What do you think?"

"Hot!" he managed at last. He felt the heat burning all the way down his throat and settling somewhere in his chest.

"Of course it's hot, you baghead. It's right from the pot. But is it good?" She asked the question as if she knew the answer already, as if she dared him to make any judgment other than a positive one.

"It's good," he said, pushing his bag aside and rubbing his chest. "It's very good."

"Of course it is," she nodded. "But it needs a bit more skkargon." She reached up over her head to a shelf of crocks. There were no labels on any of them, but she did not waste time sorting. She knew exactly where the spice was. Skkargon. Jakkin shuddered. That would make the mash even hotter. Skkargon was compounded of burnwort and something else. He opened his mouth and breathed in and out deeply. The aftertaste of the mash was wonderfully full on his tongue.

"Is that dinner?" he asked, suddenly hopeful.

"This? Of course not. I'll let it cool and put it down in the cellar in a big crock. In a couple of weeks it'll set and we can spread it on hot buns or slabs of bread." She spoke even as she threw two handfuls of skkargon into the mash and stirred. Without looking up at him, she added, "But if you are recovered enough to eat something solid, you'll find extra slabs of meat in the box." Her head jerked towards a series of metal lockers standing against the wall.

As he walked over to them, Jakkin heard a soft humming. He knew that in the main city of Rokk, where the original masters had lived, there was electrical power in every building. But around the countryside there were only a few small generators. The starships still landed in Rokk and rumor was that, from time to time, they brought a few extra generators to the planet. Jakkin had never seen one. He wouldn't even know what one looked like. He put his hand onto the first lockers and could feel a buzzing under his fingers. He looked up at Kkarina, ready to ask her about it, but she was tasting the mash, her eyes closed, lips moving in and out as if answering her own questions.

He opened the first locker. It was cold inside and little puffs of mist as fine as dragon's breath formed around the door. On the shelves jars stood in silent rows. The jars were filled with red and orange liquids of varying viscosities. The next locker was equally cold. It contained loaves of bread. Jakkin found the meat in the third cold locker. He took out a bright pink slab and carried it over to the stove.

Kkarina, her eyes open now, put the spoon back into the mash and laughed at him. As she stirred, she said, "Sit down and eat. A long hunger makes a short appetite."

Jakkin sat, wrapping his legs around the stool legs, and chewed contentedly. As he thought about the cold lockers, he was distracted by the strong juices in the meat. Soon all he concentrated on was the flow of the juice into his mouth, the passage of meat down his throat. He didn't say a word until he had finished the slab, and then all he could manage was a quiet "Thank you."

Kkarina hummed an old melody as she worked. Jakkin recognized it as the song "The Little

Dragon of Akkhan." He did not know all the words. He was just wondering if he dared ask for another piece of meat when Kkarina turned to him.

"Take another slab with you, and then off to bed. You look ready to fall, boy."

Jakkin was about to thank her again, when he noticed something peculiar. Without meaning to, he framed a statement that was part question. "But you wear no bag."

"So?"

"But a bonder . . ." He hesitated, and kept staring at her bagless neck. It was spattered with reddish-gold freckles, like her arms.

"What makes you think I'm a bonder?" She tasted another spoonful, nodding her head.

"But staying here at the Nursery. And cooking. And not living in the masters' quarters, with a single room. I just thought . . ." His voice trailed off in confusion.

"You just thought what every bond boy thinks. That a master need not work—except if he wants to play at being a nursery owner or a senator, eh? That anyone lucky enough to have gold to fill her bag would lead a useless, silly life?"

Jakkin tried to shrug, but the movement hurt his back. And he wouldn't admit to Kkarina that he had never really thought much about being a master except for filling his bag and freeing himself from bond.

"Listen, boy, I had years enough of mindlessness in the Baggeries. Where boys like you tried to become men in one slippery, sweaty night. When you're pretty, no one expects much more than open legs and a closed mind."

"*You*? In the Baggeries?" Jakkin tried to imagine it, that large, shapeless body decked out in the filmy fripperies of a Bag girl. Still, when Kkarina spoke, her voice was low and full of music.

"I'll tell you something, boy. Feeding this big family of bonders is a tough job, and I love it. Feeding them well, feeding them with the finest meals this side of Rokk. I *love* it." She smiled again and pointed to the wall. "Look at that."

His eye followed. Above the stove there was a framed miniature, a bit sooty around the edges, with a dark jagged stain, like lightning, jetting from the right side to the left. Jakkin stood up and walked over, leaning across the corner of the warm stove to see. There was a girl in the picture, beautiful and unsmiling with eyebrows as graceful and arched as dragon wings. He thought that if she were only smiling, she would have broken the heart of anyone who looked at her. As it was, the picture only called forth a kind of slow compassion.

"That was done of me when I was younger," Kkarina said. "I keep it around to remind me of the bad times."

Slowly Jakkin turned and looked at Kkarina, trying to find at least a ghost of that unsmiling beauty hidden in her flesh. His imagination was not that good, he decided at last. Only the eyebrows were the same.

"She was never happy, that girl," said Kkarina. "She didn't cry—but she never smiled either. She was never happy then, but she is now. It was Sarkkhan who helped me, bless that man. He's one who has never forgotten his past. Now go on, boy, and get yourself some more food."

Jakkin went over to the locker and took another slab. The cool air from the box was like the beginning of Dark-After. He wrapped the meat in a napkin and went out, careful to nod at Kkarina as he left.

In the bondhouse, he eased himself onto his bunk and ate the meat quickly. Then he snuggled inside his downer and closed his eyes. He reminded himself that he would have to wake up in the middle of the night, but he was sure that the noise of the others coming to bed would get through to him. And wondering vaguely if he should empty his bag to buy himself a timepiece at the Nursery store, he fell into a sleep that was completely without dreams.

7

Even before the others returned to the bondhouse, Jakkin awoke. He kept his eyes closed and listened while first the men and then the boys straggled in. If they guessed he was awake, they would try to get him to talk. But he wanted to listen and pick up information, not become involved in a long storytelling session.

The first voice he could identify belonged to Balakk, the old plowman, whose main duties were to the acres of weed and wort plants and the large kitchen garden. He was complaining, as usual.

"The river's going dry again if we don't get some rain. I've told Master Sarkkhan we'd better drill. There's water down below. I know it."

An answering grunt did not identify Balakk's partner.

"Plenty of water below. Even the worms smell it. I tell you, I fill my bag, and I'm leaving this Nursery, lest Master Sarkkhan start drilling. Got to have more reliable water than this."

Jakkin could hear Balakk's fist striking his hand, but he also knew that Balakk would not leave. The tall gaunt plowman had been making one complaint, one threat after another for twenty years. It was said of him that he loved complaining and farming in equal measure and that, hidden away somewhere, he had gold enough to fill his bag fifty times over.

Other voices cut across Balakk's complaint, coming closer to Jakkin's bed, finally drowning out the old man's argument. Even seeing Jakkin with his eyes closed did not stop the talkers. After all, a bonder was supposed to be able to sleep through anything.

"Shh. Maybe we should . . ." That had to be Errikkin. Only Errikkin would try to hush the bonders. Then, as if he had seen something on the faces of the others, Errikkin's voice changed. "Of course Jakkin can sleep with dragons fighting over him."

"On him," amended Slakk with a laugh.

There was general laughter then. Jakkin allowed himself to groan and turn over. The laughter increased.

The bantering went on for several minutes more, then the lights flickered. Even through

61

closed eyes, Jakkin could see the lights dim. In five minutes, they would go out altogether.

Jakkin waited for night to claim the room before he opened his eyes. Slowly he became accustomed to the dark, could pick out the shadows of beds, of bodies. Once or twice the door opened as a late-nighter sneaked into the room. There was surprisingly little talk, mostly about old Likkarn's being broken back to stallboy. The story of Sarkkhan and the bag was told again, and a new piece of information added.

"He didn't lose his single room. Even Master Sarkkhan would not dare put that worm waste in here with us," said Balakk. He had proudly refused a single room each year it had been offered. *"We'll* not have a weeder in here." It was the last coherent sentence Jakkin heard. A few fragments drifted around the room, and then the air pulsed with heavy breathing and the light snores of sleepers.

Jakkin waited another half hour before rising. In the dark, the aching in his shoulders and back seemed multiplied. He suppressed a groan and stood. Carrying his sandals, he tiptoed out the door. If anyone saw him, they would suspect he was meeting a girl. Maybe even Akki. He smiled at the thought. Of all the bond girls at the Nursery, she was the best-looking by far. And the only one who stayed apart. He went out of the bond-house into the night.

At first the night seemed quiet, but then Jakkin began to distinguish sounds. The *pick-buzz* of nightwings flittering around the eaves of the barn, the occasional grunting of a stud settling in his stall. Jakkin drifted towards the incubarn. Suddenly he sensed rather than heard the silent-winged approach of a drakk, the snakeheaded, deadeyed eggsucker so despised and feared by dragon breeders. As he looked up, it flew across Akkhan, its great wingspread momentarily blotting the moon from sight. He would have to report it in the morning, even though it meant exposing his own night wandering. If there was a colony of drakk nearby, it would have to be wiped out. Hundreds of eggs from one hatching could be lost to a single drakk family. The large adult drakk preyed on hatchlings, too, tearing off wings, legs, huge hunks of flesh from the living young with their razored talons. For good reason, there was a high bounty on drakk. Jakkin waited until the monster was gone from sight. It would not be back until Dark-After was past, since it had just checked the area with its sensors.

In the Nursery, a hen dragon stomped her feet at Jakkin's approach, but he did not fear her roaring out. Once the nestlings were hatched, the hens were usually quiet at night, wrapped contentedly around their squirming charges. They chewed burnwort and drizzled the juices into their hatchlings' mouths. For the first month of life, after the hatchlings grew out of their eggskins, they would exist on nothing but the juice. Their little red toothbuds would grow into sharp, white points, and then the hatchlings, too, could chew the leaves of blisterweed and wort, grinding out the juices for themselves and then following the juice with the mashed leaves for bulk.

Jakkin reached the door of the barn and, standing in a shadow, looked around. There was no one in sight. He lifted the latch and went in.

In the half-light supplied by the sulfur lamp, he made his way down the narrow halls. Unlike the stud barn, where wide hallways accommodated the cock dragons, these halls were used only for the human workers. Each compartment for the female and her brood had two doors, one small door opening into the hall and one wide door to the outside. The incubarn was a low, round building built around a central mow, a single column that supported the roof. Around the column was a hollow frame of slats which served as a ventilator to discharge the steam from the packed weed and wort leaves. Jakkin had once heard someone comment that the steam rising up was sometimes so dense you could wash your hands in it. At the top of the roof, the steam was caught in a series of vents that passed back through the barn to keep

64

the individual compartments warm, even in the cold of Dark-After. It was thought that the warmer the hatchlings were kept, the faster and bigger they grew.

The workers' walkway was in between the central mow and the hens' compartments. Sweat began to trickle under Jakkin's arms, but the heat from the mow felt good on his back. It eased the ache.

Jakkin went first to the eggroom, where all the clutches were kept together for hatching. He knew at once that the hatching was finished, because the room was completely dark, but he went back into the hall and borrowed a lamp anyway and returned. Little round shadows pitted the walls as the lamp lit the broken shells. Jakkin kicked through the sand floor, smashing pieces of the brittle casings. Jakkin knew, as any nursery bonder knew, about shells. When they were laid, they were elastic, cascading out onto the birth sands in numbers too plentiful to count. They piled up in great slippery pyramids that stuck together with birth fluids during the ice-cold of Dark-After. Only when the temperatures on the planet rose again, and the fluids melted, did the eggs drop from the pyramids into the sand. That was another reason why the barn was kept heated, to hasten the hatching process.

Jakkin knew that, touched then, the eggs would break open, revealing a viscous, yellow-green slime. Yet left alone the eggs hardened in a day, sheathed in a covering that even a sharpened pick could hardly open—from the outside. The growing hatchling within could break apart the shell with a horny growth on its nose. So once the egg had hardened, it was considered fair game for any human—thief, trainer, man, or boy—who thought he could sense a living dragon in the shell.

The living dragon. That was the irony. So few of the eggs held living dragons. Most were decoys for the predatory drakk. How often a bonder had had an opportunity to steal an egg, guarding it zealously, only to discover days later that it contained a heavy liquid and nothing else.

The shells were brittle now because the hens had licked the insides clean of the remaining birth fluids. One by one, the bonders had led the hens in to choose their own hatchlings and suck some sustenance from the sticky fluids. He could see the prints of hen feet in the sand. Angrily, Jakkin kicked at the shells. Then he bent down and picked one up, crunching it in his hand, delighting in the pain as parts of one scratched his palm, drawing blood. "Fewmets," he cursed, and stood.

He knew he should go back to the bondhouse. Stealing an egg was one thing, a kind of acceptable thievery. Stealing a hatchling—that was something else. Eggs were not counted, but hatchlings were, counted and recorded and set down in Likkarn's careful script on the doorway of each hen's nestroom. He had never seen it, but he knew it was so, just as he knew about eggs. It was part of every Nursery bonder's knowledge, the rules and lore with which he had grown up.

He knew what he *should* do, but something drew him towards the nestrooms, some thin thread of sound. It was the peeping of a hatchling and the snuffling answer of the hen. He closed the eggroom door and moved on down the hall.

At the first hen's compartment, he read Likkarn's list out loud. "Heart Worm (4) out of Heart Safe by Blood Bank. M. Blood Brother. 7 hatchlings, 5/27/07."

He lifted the latch and, holding the lamp overhead, stared in. Heart Worm was a yellowish color, not much darker than the eggskin of a newborn. She looked back at him with shrouded eyes and houghed in warning.

Jakkin squatted back on his heels and sang in that low croon, "It's all right, mother worm. It's all right."

She put her head back down and nuzzled the seven dragonlings one by one. Jakkin counted with her, saying the numbers in the same low voice. He watched her tail. The tip twitched back and forth, but he could tell that she was made only slightly anxious by his presence. He stood up slowly and backed out of the door.

The second hen was Heart to Heart, also out of

Heart Safe by Blood Bank. She was a yellow orange with a deep streak of red from her muzzle to her hindquarters. It spread like a bloodstain over her legs, then spattered like scores (or, Jakkin thought, like Kkarina's freckles) along her tail. She curled around five hatchlings, two of them still fully covered with eggskin. That meant he had missed the last of the hatchlings by only a day. Jakkin bit his lip as disappointment welled up.

Heart to Heart was even calmer than her sister had been. She barely raised her head when he entered. Jakkin took advantage of this and moved to her side, crooning to her the whole while. He put out his hand carefully and stroked the nearest of the hatchlings, a mottled little squirmer who jumped at his touch and struck at his fingers with still-soft claws. "Thou wilt be a fighter," Jakkin whispered. The best trainers, he knew, spoke *thee* and *thou* to their dragons. It was supposed to bring them closer. He had never actually tried it with the big stud dragons. He had never thought of them as *his*. He wondered if it mattered that he did not know how to speak *thee* and *thou* correctly, having only played at it with some of the other boys. Then he laughed at himself. After all, would the dragon know if he made a mistake? Would it care?

He must have been laughing out loud, because the little dragon stared at him for a long moment.

68

Then it turned its back on him and snuggled against its mother.

Jakkin thought about the hatchling, but he could not bring himself to take it. He got up and left the room.

The next hen was Heart O'Mine, and he could hear her tail beating on the floor, an unmistakable warning. He lifted the latch anyway and slipped in. Her card said she was a half-sister to the other two hens, out of Heart Safe by Blood Type. It must have been from Blood Type's very last mating. The old stud was past mating age now, and kept somewhere far away, the other bonders said, on another farm that Sarkkhan owned. Jakkin recalled the stories of Blood Type, the fabled fighter from Sarkkhan's Nursery, his first male dragon. Fifty fights and forty-seven wins, the last a five-hour battle with a champion from the other side of the planet. Heart O'Mine had nine hatchlings this time, her second clutch. There had been a large number 2 next to her name. Nine hatchlings was a lot, especially for a second clutch. And by the sound of her tail, she was a nervous mother.

Jakkin squatted down on his heels and began the crooning that had worked so well with the first two hens, but Heart O'Mine's tail kept up its loud, irritated thumping. It was then he thought of the silly lullaby that he had sung to Blood Brother.

"*Little flame mouths,*" he began singing, swaying a bit as he did.

The hen's tail seemed to catch his beat.

"Cool your tongues," Jakkin continued.

The tail was definitely moving in time to the song.

"Dreaming starts soon, furnace lungs."

By the song's end, the hen was quieted and Jakkin sighed. A strange peeping from the corner answered him. He saw a small yellowish hatchling there, one of its wings dragging.

"Oh, you poor thing," he murmured. It must have been hurt in the hatching. Or perhaps the hen had rolled over on it one night. It would never make a fighter. It would probably end up in the Stews. A lot of people liked the meat of hatchlings. They were said to be much tenderer then old dragons. Jakkin had never tasted one.

Counting the injured hatchling as one, he numbered the rest as they squirmed closer to Heart O'Mine. He found the other eight easily.

"Bonder's luck," he whispered to the hen. "All bad." Heart O'Mine stirred at his voice. She was a strange, dark dragon with a yellowish lump above her right ear. He was wondering why Sarkkhan would breed a dragon with a deformity, when the lump moved. It stretched its oversized wings clumsily and opened its mouth to peep. No sound came out.

Jakkin was so startled he could scarcely move. His eyes made the round again. The one injured dragon in the corner, and eight at the hen's side.

That made nine, and there was still the one new-born, wrinkled and yellow as custard scum. Ten. But the card outside had said nine. He was sure of it. Could Likkarn have made a mistake? Could Master Sarkkhan? He rose slowly and backed to the door, slipped through the crack, and held the lamp up to the list. "Heart O'Mine (2) out of Heart Safe by Blood Type. M. Blood Brother. 9 hatchlings, 5/29/07."

He went back into the hen's room and counted another time to be sure. On the third count, when he had reached ten again, he sat all the way down on the floor, put the lamp by his side, and let out a sound that was somewhere between a sigh and a moan. At the sound, the hen's head came up suddenly and the little dragon slid around her ear and down her nose, tumbling end over end into the sand at Jakkin's feet. It stood up shakily, stretched its wings again, and put its head to one side as if considering him. Then it trotted awkwardly over to him. Its wings were as yet too big for its body, and the weight of them dragging in the sand was so comical, Jakkin had to put his hand up over his mouth to keep from laughing out loud.

As the hatchling moved directly into the pool of light, Jakkin could see that under its yellow egg-skin was a darker shadow.

"Thou," Jakkin said quietly to the hatchling in a awed voice. "Thou wilt be a red some day."

At his voice, the little dragon looked up and

tried a hindfoot rise. Its heavy wings pulled it over onto its back, where its tiny legs raked ineffectually at the air. Jakkin leaned over and without thinking picked it up in his hands. The little dragon stood unsteadily and sniffed about his fingers, totally unafraid. It found the scratch from the eggshell and licked at the blood. Then it lifted its head and stared at Jakkin.

Jakkin stared back into its shiny black eyes and thought he saw a movement there.

"Thou," he said again in a hushed voice and suddenly felt a small rainbow moving in his head. It was the dragon. He had reached its mind. Jakkin drew his hands closer, up to his face, and he and the dragon stared eye to eye. The rainbow in his head danced, shooting off pale bursts of color.

Heart O'Mine gave a short, sharp hough. Her tail began its warning dance on the floor. Tucking the dragon hatchling in the crook of his elbow and cradling it against his chest, Jakkin picked up the lamp with the other hand. "You have your nine, great mother," he said to the hen. "This *one* is mine. I shall make this one a great fighter. I swear it."

He slipped back into the hallway, hung the lamp up, and pushed the door shut with his shoulder. Then he went out into the night.

8

The shock of the night air, cool in comparison with the moist heat of the barn, made Jakkin shiver. The hatchling gave an answering shiver against his chest.

"There, there, little one. There, there, beauty," he said, and slipped the trembling snatchling inside his shirt. Its soft little nails caught in his skin but tickled rather than hurt, and he could feel its heart beating rapidly. He decided to keep it wrapped up until they reached the oasis.

Crossing a stone weir, one of many catch basins for the Narrakka waters, Jakkin listened again for sounds. Then he scrambled up the embankment and headed out across the sands. He traveled partly by instinct, partly by star reckoning, and cursed the light of Akkhan that was in its brightest phase. He had to get away from the Nursery line of sight before Akka, the second moon, filled the sky as well, for then it would be as light as day, at least for a little while.

There was another way to get to the oasis. It meant going down the road almost a kilometer and then striking out across the sand. But it took longer. He did not have the time.

The dragon was quiet—sleeping, he would guess—and he stroked it lightly with one finger as he kept it cradled against his chest. Then suddenly he stopped. This was not the end—but the beginning. He had the dragon that he had prayed for, longed for, worked for, but now the hard part began.

He wondered briefly how there could have been such a mistake in the count, ten hatchlings instead of the nine listed. Perhaps they hadn't added in the one with the broken wing. If so, they would know at once that one was gone. Or perhaps this one, so obviously a newborn, with its eggskin still a bright creamy color and wrinkles even on its wrinkles, perhaps this had been a last-minute egg laid by Heart O'Mine in her own compartment instead of in the eggroom. A single. He had never heard of any such thing happening before. But then, he did not know *everything* about dragons. He laughed at himself softly. Everything? Why, he realized, he scarcely knew *anything*. Except fewmets. And did he know fewmets! He laughed again. The dragon stirred under his fingers.

"*Thou*," he thought fondly, and was rewarded with a faint rainbow. "Thou art a beauty." He began to walk again.

He approached the oasis from the southwest, and under the white eye of Akkhan it suddenly looked very large. He sat down inside the reed shelter and reached into his shirt. He had to detach the little dragon's claws from his bond bag. "There, there, let it be. I fill my bag myself," he said. Then smiling, he added, "Actually, if thou art a mighty fighter, thou wilt fill it for me. But not yet. Not quite yet."

He set the hatchling on the sand and watched it stretch. It began to stumble about, investigating its new surroundings. Enticed by the moonlight, it stuck its nose out of the shelter and seemed to sniff the air. Then it stalked over to the shelter wall and made a pounce on a shadow reed that moved across the sand. Finding nothing beneath its claws, it walked to Jakkin, wings dragging slightly. Jakkin flopped over on his stomach, his head close to the dragonling. With a tentative front foot it batted at his nose. When he did not move, it struck out again, with a greater swing, and this time connected.

"Worm waste," Jakkin cried, "that stings."

His loud voice startled the hatchling and it

leaped back, moving its wings furiously and rising half an inch from the ground.

"Thou canst *fly*!" Jakkin said in a softer voice filled with awe. But the little dragon settled down at once and did not try that particular maneuver again.

"Well, come here, then," Jakkin said at last and picked up the hatchling in his hands. He was surprised anew at how soft its skin was. It looked as if it should be slippery. It was certainly not the hard brilliance of a fully scaled-out worm. Rather it was as soft as bag leather. Jakkin suddenly wondered what his own bag was made of. As suddenly, he decided he did not want to know.

He lay on his back, heedless of the little rivers of pain in his shoulders, and let the dragon walk about on his chest. Even with its soft claws, it managed to make some scratches through his shirt, but Jakkin did not mind. He thought of himself as being blooded by the dragon, just as one day the dragon itself would be blooded in the Pit.

"Then thou shalt roar, little beauty," he said to the snatchling. "When thy life's blood first spills on the sand, then thou shalt roar for the first time, full and fierce. And the bettors will know thee for a mighty fighter. Then gold will fill our bag. And I will be a man. A man, my snatchling. And I will roar with thee, my flyer, my wonder worm, my beauty lizard."

The dragon slipped down his chest, gouging a small runnel into his armpit, and landed with all four feet firmly planted in the sand. There it promptly lost interest in Jakkin, went back into the shelter, curled up, and went to sleep.

Jakkin edged closer to it and curled around it, lending it the warmth of his own body for a while. Soon he, too, slept.

The cold woke him, the beginning of the bone-numbing cold of Dark-After. Jakkin crawled out of the hut on his hands and knees and stared at the sky. He could see neither moon, only the wash of white-gold that signified the start of the false dawn.

Bonders said, "Dark-After, nothing after." Very few had ever managed to remain outdoors, even with strong constitutions and a lot more clothes on than Jakkin was wearing. The early settlers, masters and bonders alike, had stayed in their starships until housing had been built: strong stone buildings in the 150 acres that was Rokk, for the wardens and guards, cruder shelters outside Rokk's walls for the convicts. Though Jakkin had never been to the city, it was said those buildings still stood, two hundred years later, a testimony to the first Austarians. The worst punishment of the masters in the old days, before the shelters, had been to lock out a bonder all night. That was why

77

Master Sarkkhan's nursery doors were never locked—just in case. And why the roads to the Baggeries, the Stews, and the Pits were spotted with shelters, for late-nighters caught away from home.

Jakkin scrambled to his feet. He gazed once at the little dragon curled asleep in the sand. The cold would not bother it, not even as a newborn. He knew that. But just to be sure, he took off his shirt and wrapped it around the sleeping mite, placing it far back against the rear wall of reeds. Then, hugging his leather jerkin to him, he ran as fast as he could across the sand towards the Nursery. If he kept moving, he thought he could keep warm. If he ran fast enough, he could make it back before the worst of the cold struck. He would not bother about brooming his footsteps, but trust to the wind and pray to whatever god still watched over bond boys. Certainly the masters' god would not recognize him yet.

The sand seemed to slip away from his feet, making running even more difficult. Several times he stumbled and one time went crashing to his knees. It was hard to keep moving in the cold. The metal bond chain around his neck felt as if it were on fire, it was so cold, and the metal eyelets on his jerkin felt as though they were burning small holes wherever they touched his skin.

The cold made him want to stop and snuggle

down in the sand, to build himself an earth mound and sleep. Yet he knew such a sleep would be the sleep of death. *Dark-after, nothing after,* he reminded himself, his feet moving even when his mind willed them to stop.

And then his feet were running on packed earth, and he realized he was on Nursery property. But the cold befuddled him, and he was not sure where. His breath plumed out before him. He felt he could almost break it off and use it as a pick. Stick it on his forehead and break his way out of the egg of cold that surrounded him. He was sure his skin was becoming as hard and scaled as any lizard's. If blooded, he would roar. He found himself roaring, roaring, roaring, and he fell hard against a stone wall.

A gloved hand pulled at him, and he was suddenly wrapped in someone's downer.

"Hush. You're found. But the cold has snapped you. Just come along."

He thought he knew that voice. It came from another dream he had had.

A door opened and shut and the warmth made him hurt all over.

"Akki, what are you doing in here?" A sleepy voice.

"Bringing home a body."

"Why, it's Jakkin. Hey, Errikkin, look. It's Jakkin."

"Wonder where he's been all night."

"Look at his chest. Wonder what her name was?"

"Does he look different?"

"Like a man, you mean?" someone snickered.

"Was he coming from town?" A laugh. "You know."

A woman's laugh. "Yes, from the Baggeries. Can't you see? His bag is only half full."

"Or half empty." More laughs.

"I heard him roaring outside the hospice. I grabbed a blanket, threw on my own thermals, and ran."

"Lucky for him."

"He's all luck. It's a wonder he's a bonder."

Jakkin opened his eyes. His body was too hot now. He threw the blanket off. He stared at Akki, who gave him a wry smile.

"Yes," she said, staring at him. "He's had himself quite a night." She winked.

They led him to his bed and he fell asleep, murmuring "Beauty. You beauty." He heard them laugh once again before he was totally out.

9

Morning seemed to come too swiftly, summoned by the clanging breakfast bell. Jakkin could scarcely rise, and had to be dressed by Slakk and Errikkin. They did it good-naturedly and even tried to joke with him. Then they force-marched him down the hall to the common room.

It was the cup of *takk* flooding through him that gave Jakkin the strength to talk. "Did I . . . say anything in my sleep?" he asked, deciding that caution was less important than knowledge.

"Not her name," said Slakk, taking his face out of his bowl for the moment. "Nor the sign of her Baggery."

"Baggery?" Jakkin was confused.

"Oh, leave him," Errikkin said. "Maybe he

doesn't know her name. Maybe it wasn't so important."

"Any time you stay out so late the cold snaps you, and you leave your shirt behind, *it's important!*" said Slakk. The boys at the table laughed with him. Jakkin blushed, which made them laugh even more.

"I wasn't . . ." he began, and stopped. Better they guessed wrong than guessed where he *really* was.

Slakk heard his hesitation and stared at him slyly. "Unless, of course," he said, a grin starting across his face, "unless it was . . . Akki." As Jakkin made a stuttering protest, Slakk pounced. "It was. Akki." He beat his spoon on the table and began chanting "Akki, Akki, Akki."

The rest of the boys at the table joined in, even Errikkin. "Akki. Akki. Akki."

"Stop it!" Jakkin shouted angrily. "It's not Akki. Stop it." But there was no breaking through their noise. He glanced quickly over at the pair-bonders' table, but Akki was not there. Had she heard and left? Or was she not yet at breakfast?

"Akki. Akki. Akki." The boys' chant continued unabated. Now they were all beating their spoons on the table.

Jakkin jumped up and stormed from the room, slamming the door behind him. He knew his dramatic exit would make them surer, but he hadn't known what else to do. He needed time to think, time to calm down. As he pushed through the outer door and into the yard, the bright sun made him squint. The barns seemed to shimmer and glow, heat streams rising from them. The one spikka tree in the courtyard center cast a shadow but no shade. He thought of the shadows of the night before, as he had gone, bent over, towards the incubarn.

And then, suddenly, he remembered the silent-winged eggsucker that had skimmed across the face of the moon. The drakk. He had not yet reported it. It and its family, maybe even a colony, would be somewhere close by. The dragon eggs were hatched, no longer in any danger, but there were still the hatchlings to consider. Soon the hens and hatchlings would be let out into the henyard. A drakk with its sharp, curved talons could maim or kill an unprotected hatchling before the hen was even aware of the drakk's presence. Drakk were silent, and—alive—they had no smell. Dead, they covered anyone close by with a heavy, nauseating odor of decay. Jakkin had heard that a drakk family on the hunt would circle endlessly, taunting a hen until she was drawn away from her helpless brood into a fruitless chase. He thought of his own dragon, his little beauty, out alone in the reeds.

"Stay in the shelter till I come for thee," he murmured, knowing that his thoughts could not reach so far, but hoping that the young snatchling's instincts would keep it in the shelter for a while.

He turned and went back towards the bond-house. As he went in the door, he was relieved to find that the chanting was over.

One of the younger boys, red-haired Trikko, started to call out when he saw Jakkin: "Akk—" He was stopped with an elbow in the stomach by Errikkin, who then turned and, immediately contrite, asked if Trikko had been hurt.

Jakkin nodded at his friends and walked over to the table where the older men sat: Balakk and his two helpers were there, as well as Jo-Janekk, who ran the Nursery store, and Frankkalin, who was the main toolsmith and mason. At one corner of the table, surrounded by a self-imposed silence, sat Likkarn. The others ignored him and he glowered into his food bowl. Likkarn looked up only once and stared at Jakkin with such a look of distaste that Jakkin could feel a cold band of sweat start on his neck. He put his hand up to wipe it off and at the same time greeted the other men. He dried his hand on the side of his pants.

"Well, boy?" It was Balakk.

"Last night . . ." Jakkin began.

"Oh, we heard about your late night," chuckled Jo-Janekk, smoothing his moustache with one hand. "Woke the whole bond house, you did."

Jakkin's hand went up to his bag and he squeezed it, letting the tension flow out of his fingers onto the familiar soft bag surface. "Last night," he continued, "a drakk flew overhead. Near the henyard."

Likkarn looked up again. The distaste still showed in his eyes. "A drakk? Are you sure?" he asked quickly.

"Do you know what you're saying? What a drakk hunt will mean to the schedule here on the farm?" added Balakk.

"It was a drakk," Jakkin said, hoping they would not question him more.

"Describe it," said Likkarn, standing up and coming over to him. His red-rimmed eyes glistened. He was close enough so that Jakkin could see the gray and black beard stubble breaking through the scarred surface of his face.

Jakkin took a breath.

"What you *saw*, bonder," Likkarn added. "Not what you expected to see."

"It was a shadow. A black, silent shadow overhead. Wings stretched so." He spread his arms. "And a long snaky shadow of a head."

"A drakk," Balakk complained.

"Flying which way?" Likkarn asked, as if he did not believe a word.

Jakkin closed his eyes and saw again the great wings of the drakk. "Flying east to west, from beyond the bondhouse towards the incubarn."

"Fewmets!" Balakk's fist slammed against the table. "Those pieces of lizard waste seem to grow out of nothing. Nothing! I've a mind to quit farming and take a job in Rokk. I thought we had wiped them out seven years ago."

Likkarn's lips moved in and out purposefully. "Sometimes a new colony starts when the young are forced out by their elders," he said. "Out to find new territory . . . and new food. Across the desert sands, closer to civilization." He glared at Jakkin.

"And we were going to take the hatchlings out this very evening for their first airing," said Crikk, Balakk's right hand and his closest friend. He was a young man, just out of childhood, his arms pitted with blood scores. He had helped Sarkkhan several times in the Minor Pits before asking to be transferred back to the farm. "We don't dare take them out now. They'd just be meat for those monsters."

"So it's a hunt, then," said Balakk wearily. "A regular de-bagged roundup."

"Well, I've got plenty of knives, but they'll need honing," Frankkalin said as he rose. "I'll take some of the boys and get started." He went over to the table and fingered Errikkin, his special favorite, and two of the younger boys. They followed him silently; his one-word explanation was enough.

"I'll start Slakk and the other boys on the dragon food. The baths will have to wait until this is over," Likkarn said. Any sign of weed in his eyes was now gone. "I'll meet you back here in an hour.

You take the boy" he signaled with his chin at Jakkin "and chart that flight."

Likkarn left, dragging Slakk and the others behind him.

"He acts as if he's still head here," complained Kkittakk, Balakk's second helper, a bonder new to the Nursery. "And he's only a lower stallboy now."

"You've not been here long enough to know," Balakk said. "When it comes to fighting drakk, I'll stand behind Likkarn any day. He's got a nose for them, he has. He's as bloody-minded as they are. I remember once he fought a drakk barehanded . . . but there's time to tell that later." Balakk stood up. "Come, boy, show me where you saw that piece of worm waste. We'll have to take soundings." He sighed loudly and unfolded his long body from the bench.

They followed Balakk into the hall, where he unlocked a free-standing cupboard full of instruments. He took out a metal and glass object and polished the base of it with his sleeve. Then, finding a package of soft material in the cupboard, he polished the glass lens as well.

"There, that'll do for a first sounding. Now show me exactly where you were when that piece of filth passed over."

In the courtyard, Jakkin stood still for a moment, remembering. "It was night," he said softly.

"We *know* that," Kkittakk complained.

"Hush, you bonder, or I'll de-bag what little

you've got," Balakk said in a fierce whisper. "He means it was dark out and he has to re-feel where he stood. Fewmets, man, this thing is going to be hard enough without your interruptions."

Grateful for Balakk's support, Jakkin closed his eyes. He was worried. If he told them exactly where he had been, he might give away the stealing of the dragon, for he had been on the path to the incubarns. But if he lied, the charting of the flight would be off by a kilometer or more, and the drakk might never be found. He thought what that could mean, picturing a hatchling squirming and peeping its fear, hot dragon blood dripping down where the talons gripped, scoring the sand below. He suddenly saw his own dragon with its life spilling out on the sands. He knew then there was no choice.

"Here," he said. "I was walking here. And the drakk flew this way." His hand cut through the air in a steady trajectory. It dipped once, just as the drakk's wings had dipped going by his head, and pointed to a spot well beyond the Nursery, out in the sands.

Balakk grunted and turned the wheels of the instrument in his hand. He shouldered Jakkin aside and stood where Jakkin had stood, sighting through the eyepiece.

"There's a copse of spikka trees directly in line. And four or five kilometers further is the edge of

Sukker's Marsh. If we have to go in there to find them, it might take days."

"And back, where it flew from?" Jakkin asked dismally, for that way lay the sands in which his own dragon was hidden.

"I'll get to that. I will." Balakk turned, and sighted along the flight line. "No trees on the flight line. It's far and away across the sands before you come to anything in which a family of those baggy horrors could roost. Lucky for us they fly in such straight trajectories. Except when they're on the hunt. But with the dragons all inside right now, they'd just be making their regular straight passes. When they're hunting they can scent a dragon up to five kilometers on either side of their path and straight down as well. They have scent sensors along their bodies, covered by the wings."

Jakkin nodded, the tightness in his chest relaxing only slightly.

"How big were its wings?" Balakk asked again.

Jakkin spread his arms apart a little, then further.

"A small one. Pray to the gods they're all that size. I heard of a man who tackled a really big drakk, one with a wingspread longer than I'm high. Near dragon-size, it was. Ripped him open as easily as a nestling pecks out of its egg." Balakk shuddered. "Let's hope they're all small ones. And that Frankkalin can get his knives honed sharp.

We'll take the extinguishers, too. Sarkkhan needs to be told. Jo, you do that. And we'll all have to get into leathers. It's some protection at least."

"In this heat?" Kkittakk began.

"Ripped him from here," Balakk said easily, pointing to just under his throat, "to here." He finished drawing a line down to his groin.

Kkittakk nodded. "Leathers it is," he said.

They walked back to the bondhouse in silence, while Jo-Janekk disappeared towards Sarkkhan's sandbrick house. It was on a small rise overlooking the entire Nursery and was surrounded by twenty-year trees. Jakkin had never been inside. Few of the bonders had. Master Sarkkhan was a solitary man who spent time training the pit fighters, running them in the Major Pits, or off on his other farm with the retired studs. He was rarely at the Nursery—and never entertained there. He gave orders—and the orders were passed along. Jakkin knew him by sight and by the sound of his voice, a big, booming gong of a voice. He doubted if Sarkkhan knew much about him.

The drakk fighters met outside in less than an hour, dressed in leathers. Jakkin, being the youngest and unfamiliar with the Pits, had never owned his own coveralls. He wore a pair of fawn-colored ones that Jo-Janekk had found for him. They were too long and had to be rolled up. There were several strange scarrings on the legs. Jakkin did not ask where the deep scratches came from. He was afraid he knew. He was grateful, though, that they let him be part of the roundup. Some bonders felt that a successful roundup changed a boy into a man. Jakkin was grateful and, though he wouldn't admit it out loud, very frightened. He had heard a lot about drakk, none of it good.

"Master Sarkkhan was not in his house. He's away at the Pits," Jo-Janekk began.

"Fewmets, that's right," Balakk cursed. "I forgot. He's got two fighters. Hoping to have a winner at the Minor Pits with them. He's hungry, is Master Sarkkhan. Hasn't had a winner in months. Not even at a Minor. Well, I hope he has them today, or that we find those pieces of waste. Otherwise, I'd not bet a coin to fill a dead man's bag against a sack of gold but that he'll have us on half rations before nightfall."

"Now, Bal," Jo-Janekk began, "you know he's not that kind of master. He came up from bond himself."

"The worst kind are gold masters, they say," Kkittakk put in. "Worse than born masters."

"You haven't been here long enough to know," said Frankkalin.

"Save your fire for the drakk," Likkarn warned them. "We can't wait till Sarkkhan comes back, win or no win." He rubbed his hand over the bib of his coverall, touching the place where his bag lumped. "You can't wait with drakk flying out there." He looked at Jakkin. "Do we have to take this bag of waste?"

"Yes." Balakk gave the answer without hesitation, and as he was now Senior, Likkarn could not quarrel with him.

Jakkin could feel the cold sweat begin again, beading his neck and running down the crease of his back. He wondered that he could feel so cold when he should be hot in the confining leathers.

Wordlessly, Frankkalin gave out the knives. Long, straight-bladed, they resembled machetes with bone handles. Each man got one. Likkarn, Balakk, and Frankkalin carried extinguishers as well, the three that could be spared from the hallways.

"Stingers for stunning, but finish them with knives," Balakk cautioned. "We can't waste power. There's not another shipment of power packs due into Rokk till next year, and we're already low." He did not have to mention Likkarn's killing of Blood Brother. It was on everyone's mind.

Likkarn grunted and looked away.

Balakk continued as if there had been no interruption. "And once the drakk are down, they can be cut easily enough. Just be sure they *are* down, though, and always come at them from behind. Even a downed drakk can sometimes make a pass at you with his claws, a reflex like. Knew a man once, had his leg near took off by a drakk he thought was dead." He shivered. 'Those . . .

those . . ." even his curse words seemed inadequate. He spat to one side. "I hate them."

Though they all knew the basics of hunting drakk, no one minded the extra warning. Then Jo-Janekk handed out the masks. "Clip them to your shoulder straps and snap them on at the last," he explained. "There's no smell like a dead drakk. It'll fair incapacitate you. Let's hope we get lots of them today."

"*Drakk!*" they shouted together, lifting their knives and stingers overhead. As if the shouted word guaranteed success, they shouted it again, Jakkin louder than the rest. He put his fear into the word and hurled it from him, then pumped his arm high, catching the sunlight with the blade, "*Drakk! Drakk! Drakk!*"

The ululation continued to echo as they marched out of the yard, a band of seven in gray and tan leathers. The other bonders stood by the barn doors to watch them pass.

Jakkin wondered suddenly if Akki, too, watched from the hospice or if she was away on some errand of her own. He threw his chest out and strutted down the road like the rest.

10

The grim parade, sweating freely under the eye of Austar's red sun, marched out the two kilometers to the copse of spikka trees. Jakkin had minded well what Jo-Janekk had said to him in the bondhouse, before he had dressed in his leathers: "It is no shame to be afraid, but it is foolish to go out with a full bladder." He only wished they could stop now, but he did not dare break the silence to ask.

Likkarn gestured as they came close to the trees. He chose three hunters—Blakk, Frankkalin, and Jakkin—to circle to the right, and three—Jo-Janekk, Crikk, and Kkittakk—to the left. Likkarn's fingers signaled that he would remain at the point.

They obeyed him at once, moving on silent feet into the circle. If the drakk were flying, the men would be scented. But drakk had notoriously bad ears and eyes. If the marchers were careful, they could catch the colony by surprise just as it rose from the nests.

There were not more than forty trees in the copse, though it was a large stand by Austar standards. Being so near Sukker's Marsh meant that there was water feeding into an underground stream. Each tree would have to be approached, shaken, searched. Drakk adult males were fairly easy to spot. They always sat hunched over like dark fruit high up on the topside of the broad, spiky leaves. The females, however, squatted in the nests and had to be shaken out. And the infant drakk within the nests were the most difficult to find. The tallest trees had to be climbed; and Jakkin, being the youngest and lightest of the hunters, was to be the climber.

The ground directly under the trees was spongy. The men's steps down were silent, cushioned by the wet, sandy soil. But each time they pulled their feet up again, the sucking noise seemed as loud as a dragon's roar.

At Likkarn's signal, they stopped and listened. Then Likkarn put his fingers to his mouth, wiggled his fingers, and made a peculiar peeping sound. Jakkin was startled. He had never heard anyone call in that way. It sounded just like a dragon hatchling in trouble. The mewling cry of a nestling just out of the shell echoed around the oasis, but there was no answering hiss from a drakk on the hunt.

Jakkin looked over at Frankkalin, who mouthed back: "Daylight." Drakk did not ordinarily hunt by day. Only a rare drakk could be goaded or fooled into a day flight. But if these were young drakk, and they were in the copse and they were hungry, perhaps . . . it was a chance they had to take. Likkarn gave the cry again. It was greeted with more silence.

He gestured them forward, each to the foot of a small tree. Jakkin watched the others before tackling his own tree. First the top was scanned carefully, then the trunk was shaken. If there was no hiss from the treetop, no drakk shaken into a diving flight from the tree, a slashing X with the knife on the trunk marked it as having been searched.

They scanned and shook some twenty-seven small trees, the last two large enough to need two men for the shaking. It was all done silently.

Thirteen trees in the copse remained. They were too large and thick for shaking. They would have to be climbed.

Jo-Janekk reached into his pack and drew out two sets of pitons—knifelike clamps. One set was to be tied onto sandals and the other was already

sewn into leather gloves. Jakkin had heard of
them but he had never used them before. Jo-
Janekk showed him the best way to secure the
pitons to his shoes, and mimed the climbing, whispering in his ear, "Just find them. Don't be a hero.
Leave the rest to us. When you find them, drop
straight down and show by fingers how many."
Then he gave Jakkin a boost up the tree.

Jakkin clamped first his hand pitons, then the
feet, into the slippery-smooth gray bark of the tree.
The knives dug easily into the trunk, their thudding impact the only sound in the oasis. He began
a slow ascent, moving one arm, then one leg at a
time, rocking the knife a bit to free it from the
trunk, drawing it out, clamping it in again. He
was halfway up the tree when the first real wave
of fear hit him. If there were drakk in the toothed
leaves above him, they could rake him with their
razored claws before he could remove his knife
from his coverall belt. Rip him, he remembered
Balakk's saying, "from here"—and drawing his
hand down to below his stomach—"to here." Jakkin gripped the tree with his arms as well as the
knives, closed his eyes, and could not move.

A sharp hiss from below made him open his
eyes again. It was not a drakk, but Likkarn pointing the extinguisher directly at him. Jakkin shook
his head, and Likkarn answered with a shake of
the stinger. Next to Likkarn stood Balakk, his

knife drawn, his mouth forming the words "Move, boy."

Jakkin moved. He was less afraid of the drakk than the stinger in Likkarn's hands. The drakk were only a possibility, but the narrowing of the old weeder's eyes was a certainty. Jakkin climbed.

The trunk of the spikka tree was long and criss-crossed with old knife cuts, though whether from other drakk hunts or from climbing games or from the lopping of limbs of wood, Jakkin could not be sure. The scars had healed black against the gray trunk, and already the oozing cuts his pitons inflicted upon the wood were closing behind him, a dark trail of scars. The spikka allowed little moisture to escape.

Jakkin climbed until the men below were the size of small boys. He could see that Balakk had a bald spot the size of a gold coin and that Likkarn had an egg-shaped one. His own head touched the first leaves. He stopped and scanned, peering through the ragged edges of the leaves that fanned around the treetop like a crown. His eyes saw nothing, though his heart continued to thump loudly at every shadow.

He pulled one hand loose and, balancing carefully, took the glove off his hand with his teeth. He let it drop to his chest. Then he detached the knife from the belt slipknot with an easy motion. Silently he pushed the knife up through two leaves, bending one back slowly. Now he could see the rest of the leaves clearly. There were no drakk. He put the knife between his teeth, managed to get the glove back on his hand, and went down much faster than he had gone up.

The ground felt solid and welcoming. He turned to the others and made a zero between his thumb and forefinger, saying the word silently to them, and tied his knife back on his belt. They nodded, and Balakk added a long, fresh slash of X's to the tree, chest high.

The climb up the second tree was easier, both on his muscles and his mind. He went up without stopping, scanned the leaves, and descended. The third tree was the same.

The fourth tree was longer and more fully leafed out. One leaf was blackened as if it had caught on fire. Occasionally, when the droughts were at their worst, a spikka tree had been known to burst into flame spontaneously. At first Jakkin had thought the black leaf was a drakk. He had been ready to drop from the tree like a stone. But squinting his eyes, he could make out the jagged edges, and when it did not fly off, even under prodding from his knife, he knew it was just a leaf. He climbed down slowly, his heart beating strangely in his chest.

He took some deep draughts from the water bottle Balakk proferred, and squatted back on his heels as the men whispered above him. They were trying to decide which trees seemed the most promising or the least difficult to climb.

"Are you all right, boy?" Jo-Janekk mouthed at him, ruffling his sweaty hair.

Jakkin nodded. Even with the water, his mouth was dry.

Up the fifth tree, he could feel the water sloshing in his tightened stomach, remembering too late Jo-Janekk's message about his bladder. He should have gone without the drink. He was thinking about that, and not about the climb, when his head touched the leaves and a sharp hiss caught him by surprise. He dropped by reflex, his arms up, the pitons flashing above his head. He heard the shouting of the men and the sharp retort of the stinger.

It was the awful smell, dark, penetrating, searing his nose, fighting its way down his throat, that woke him to action. He reached up to his shoulder, found the mask dangling there, and jammed it on. Several quick breaths revived him. He stripped off the gloves, grabbed up his knife, and looked around.

On the ground near him was a drakk. Its oily green snakehead was severed from its body, but the body still flapped its enormous wings, uncovering the scabrous, pulsing sensor organs. The near-blind snake eyes glowed with a dark malevolence that went out slowly like the embers of a dying fire. The talons of the body gripped and ungripped on an invisible prey.

Jakkin walked around the back of the drakk and suddenly stabbed at it with his knife. He cut into the drakk body again and again as if he could, by his actions, cut away his own fears. A viscous blood pulsed out at each cut. He jabbed at the drakk until his arm was tired. Then, finally exhausted, he stopped and looked around for the others.

The six bonders stood in a circle under the tree, knives drawn, waiting. When no other drakk flew down, Likkarn gestured them away. He walked around the tree, girdling it quickly with the stinger. The tree fell, heavily, its descent slowed by its close neighbors. At last its leafy crown was caught securely between two other trees. It hung there low enough for their knives.

The bonders moved toward the tree, circling it. Jakkin stood behind them, peering over Jo-Janekk's shoulder. Likkarn pointed with his stinger, and grunted.

In the topmost leaves was a nest of kkhan reeds plastered together with dragon fewmets. The reed tops were arranged in such a way that the nest looked exactly like a spikka leaf. Even close up, it was difficult to distinguish it. Suddenly a small snakehead peered over the side of the nest. Then another. Jakkin counted quickly. There were seven young drakk hissing furiously up at them.

They could not fly yet, and tried to hide under one another.

"Seven," called out Likkarn in a doomsday voice slightly obscured by his mask. "Be sure. Seven."

The men marched into the leaves and stabbed the squirming little horrors with their knives, severing the heads from the bodies. The drakklings died quickly, leaving the dreadful stench behind. Their thick, dark blood coated the knives and had to be washed off immediately in the sand. Even then, the blood left pits and ruts in the shine.

They buried the remains of the drakk and their nest in a great hole they dug out beneath the fallen tree. Reluctantly Jakkin climbed the rest of the trees, his knife always at the ready in his clenched teeth, but he found nothing else.

On their march back to the bondhouse for hour-long showers in hot water with strong yellow soap, Likkarn spoke only once.

"I don't like it," he said. "The female and the young. Where was the male? I don't like it."

"Perhaps she had mated before she came here," offered Crikk.

"Yes, that's it," said Kkittakk.

"Perhaps," said Balakk. But like Likkarn he was not happy.

Likkarn took out some weed and rolled it mechanically into a thin red cylinder with one hand. He had already started smoking it by the time they entered the courtyard. They left him alone and hurried into their showers.

Old Likk-and-Spittle may have been worried, Jakkin thought, but not enough to lay off the weed. So Jakkin wasn't worried either. He had dipped his knife into a drakk's blood and come out a man. Surely he was ready to tackle anything now. He thought of his dragon waiting out in the sand.

"See, thou mighty fighter," he called to it in his mind. "I am a mighty fighter, too."

At the dinner table, the talk was all about the fight with the drakk. The boys had the story from Jakkin at least three times, in three different versions. Each time the tale ended with his killing the drakk and then the hour-long attempt at scrubbing the smell from his hide.

"It lingers," said Jakkin. "Gods, how it lingers."

"You're telling me," Slakk put in, holding his nose.

Errikkin jabbed Slakk in the ribs, and they all laughed.

"And my jaw still aches from holding the knife in my teeth." Jakkin waggled his jaw at them and they nodded admiringly.

"I wish *I* had been there," Errikkin said wistfully.

Jakkin did not tell them how he had bloodied

his knife in the back of a *dead* drakk, and how wet
the inside of his coveralls had been, and how next
time, if there were a next time, he would never
take a drink in the middle of a roundup. But he
did add, "Each of the men on the march is going
to get part of the bounty. Eight drakks. I'm to
have a full seventh share." He did not have to say
a *man's* share. That was understood.

Errikkin interrupted. "You *should* get it. After
all, you were in the most danger, climbing up the
tree."

"Not really," Slakk said. "Remember, he was
dropping fast, while the others were standing still
below."

"But he was closest," said Errikkin.

The boys began to take sides, some supporting
Errikkin with great vehemence, and one or two
restating Slakk's argument. Jakkin stopped them
by banging his spoon on the table.

"Enough," he said. "What matters is that I have
filled my bag with this fight. Or at least," he
added truthfully, "a bit more gold will clink in it.
And . . ." He paused for effect.

They listened.

"And?" asked Errikkin, right on cue.

"And I have been given tomorrow as an addi-
tional Bond-Off day. I don't have to work. I can go
where I want." Jakkin spoke the words with a kind
of sly joy.

"And where will you go?" The questioner was one of the youngest boys, little L'erikk, Frank-kalin's son.

"Do you need to ask?" said Slakk. He began pounding his fist on the table. "Akki, Akki, Akki."

The others laughingly joined in.

Jakkin looked quickly over at the pair-bonders table. Since Akki was not there, he smiled and let them go on. What did it matter how wrong they were? *He* knew he would be spending first his night and then his Bond-Off day out on the sands with his dragon.

the snatchling

11

Jakkin left directly after dinner, strolling off down the road as if going toward the town for an evening at the local Stews. It was a long walk, nearly fifteen kilometers, but he shrugged off a ride with some of the others. Let them think what they liked; he had jangled his bag at them, clanking with the bounty coins. Let them make false guesses.

When he was passed by no more Nursery trucks (bought dearly, he knew, from the star traders at Rokk) and he could see no road dust deviling up from tires or feet either ahead of him or behind, Jakkin doubled back halfway, crossed the weir, and headed out over the sand.

Once, hearing the noise of a vehicle far off down the road, and seeing the telltale dust spiraling up, he had dug a quick depression in the sand and snuggled into it. But the truck roared by without stopping, and he realized that he had not really needed to hide. He was already far enough away from the road. Still, he knew that care was more important now than ever. Bending over and brooming his footsteps, he scuttled like a lizard over the ocean of sand. He noticed that his prints from the night before were gone, and he thanked the intermittent south wind for helping him keep his secret.

He reached the oasis before the first moon had lipped the horizon. That gave him four hours at the very least. Nothing stirred. The air was incredibly still. The weed and wort patch had stopped smoldering except for one lone stalk that sent a gentle puff of smoke into the air. Without wind to move it off, the smoke cloud hung around the tip of the plant. From where he stood, Jakkin could see the toothed leaves of the plant partially unrolled, maroon sap veins like road maps running through them. Tomorrow he would start crushing the most mature leaves.

A sudden little wind squalled through the patch, coming from nowhere. The leaves trembled, dipped. As quickly as it had come, the wind puffed itself out in the patch.

Jakkin smiled and went over to the reed shelter. Before he got there, a cascade of muted colors burst into his head. "Thou mighty snatchling," he cried. "Thou hast sensed my coming." He bent over, and started in, and was tripped by the dragonling.

Its size startled him. It was fully a body size larger than the night before, coming almost to his knees. Its eggskin was still the dirty yellow color, but now it was stretched taut over the dragon's growing muscle and bone. Underneath, the dark patches that he had only sensed were beginning to show through. And there were tears in the custard-scum-colored skin where the dragon had begun to molt. Inside the shelter, Jakkin found swatches of the eggskin hanging from snags on the wall. The snatchling had apparently rubbed against the reeds to ease the itching of its shedding skin.

Jakkin picked up one of the swatches of skin and pulled it between his hands. It stretched easily and had a soft, almost furry feel. When he let it go, it snapped back to its original shape.

Jakkin walked out of the shelter to the spring and took off his sandals. He put his feet into the warm water. The dragon held back, as if waiting for a signal.

"Come on then," he called to it softly, making enticing little trails in the sand with his hand.

The dragon watched his fingers for a moment, then trotted out of the shelter and pounced. It caught his hand in its mouth, and the red ridge of tooth bumps clamped down. One tooth must have already broken through, for there was a sharp piercing pain in his palm, but he did not take his hand away. "Fight, thou wonder," he said and was rewarded with another burst of color in his head. The dragon opened its mouth and backed off for a moment. Then, raising its trailing wings, it launched itself with a leap into the stream.

Jakkin was up in an instant, ready to follow the snatchling and rescue it, when he realized that it was paddling down the ribbon of water as easily as if it were a fish. He sat down again and watched it. Obviously it had tried this maneuver before. There was nothing casual or tentative in its swimming. When the dragon came to the stream's end, it climbed up through the kkhan reeds and trotted back to Jakkin's side, where it shook itself thoroughly, wetting Jakkin in the process.

"Thou didst that on purpose!" shouted Jakkin, cuffing the little dragon lightly, a love tap. The dragon, in the same spirit, tapped Jakkin back with its still-soft claws. It followed this attack by leaping onto Jakkin's chest. Jakkin tumbled back, and they rolled over and over, and down into the stream.

Jakkin paddled after the dragonling with more splashing and less grace. When they climbed out through the reeds, Jakkin took off his shirt and shorts and spread them out to dry on the sand.

"Listen," he said, "if thou art going to be such a rowdy, thou must eat to gather strength." He walked over to the weed and wort patch with the dragon at his heels. Carefully choosing a fully leafed-out stalk, he plucked three leaves. They were warm to the touch.

Back at the spring, he squeezed a leaf between his fingers. Only a little juice ran out of the veins. The dragon snuggled in his lap. Jakkin tickled it under the chin. The dragon opened its mouth and Jakkin drizzled what juice he could into its mouth and on its nose.

At first the hatchling looked surprised. Then it sent a long, red-ribbed tongue out to explore its muzzle for whatever juice remained.

Jakkin crushed the second leaf, puncturing the vein at several places with his fingernail. This time he was able to extract more juice from the plant.

The snatchling slurped it eagerly, licking Jakkin's fingers for whatever was left.

The third round of juice seemed to satisfy the dragon's hunger completely, and it fell asleep as soon as it had finished giving Jakkin's red-stained fingers a perfunctory lick.

Jakkin sat for almost an hour with the little dragon on his legs, stroking its head and working carefully at a tear in the eggskin over its left ear. He crooned old songs and hummed new melodies he made up himself. He murmured names to it. But when Akka and Akkhan sat high in the sky, making double shadows in the sand, Jakkin lifted the little dragon in his arms and carried it back into the hut. He covered it again with his old shirt.

"Sleep well, thou mighty snatchling," he whispered to it. "For I shall come to thee in the morning. And bring a bowl and bone to make thee a proper meal. I promise."

The dragon answered him only with slight, hissing snores.

Jakkin put on his clothes, now dried in the heat, and left the oasis, brooming away his trail. A slight wind, rising in the east, finished the job for him. He was back in the bondhouse and asleep long before the rest had returned from the town.

12

Bowl and bone. Those were Jakkin's very first thoughts when the morning sun streamed across his face. He was lying half in and half out of his bunk, well awake before the bell. Bowl and bone. How would he ever find them? What excuse would he use to get them?

In the end, he simply got dressed early and found his way into the kitchen before the other bonders had risen. Kkarina was stirring the *takk* in a gigantic pot, tasting it every three or four stirs.

"Good morning," Jakkin said brightly.

She turned and looked at him, raising her eyebrows but keeping her mouth on the spoon. Kkarina would never hurry her tasting. At last she finished and put the spoon back in to stir some more. "Another few minutes," she said, meaning the *takk*.

Jakkin nodded.

"Get a bowl and have a taste," she said, pointing at a small room off the kitchen.

Jakkin walked where directed and found a room of shelves with all the bowls and spoons and cutlery he could want. He slipped a bone-handled knife inside his shirt, then took a bowl and spoon and went out. It had been easy.

"Come here," Kkarina said. "You need some meat on you."

She jabbed at him with the spoon. He jumped back, and the knife inside his shirt slapped his ribs. He had a sudden fear that it would fall out. Hugging the bowl against his shirt, imprisoning the knife between it and his ribs, he went over to Kkarina.

"Drakk killer," she said affectionately, and smiled. "Hero." She touched his bag, making it jangle.

Jakkin smiled back. He knew it was a false smile and hated himself for it.

"Want to tell me the story of the hunt?"

Jakkin began the story as Kkarina filled his bowl. But when he got to the part where the mother drakk had been killed, he quickly glossed over the stabbing, not really wanting to tell Kkarina that all he had done was dip his knife into the dead drakk. But he did not want to lie to her, either. That other knife, the one under his shirt, seemed to burn a brand across his front.

"I didn't do that much," he ended lamely, remembering with shame the wet coveralls that he had stuffed into the laundry. The more he remembered, the less he wanted to remember. Some hero.

"You must have done something to have filled your bag, to have been given an extra Bond-Off."

Jakkin looked down at the full bowl. The *takk* was hot enough to send up bubbles that burst into a deep pink froth. He shrugged.

"Go on and eat. I'll pack you a lunch. Most men, after their first roundup, want to get as far away from work as possible. Must be something, that hunt." She turned her back on him and went to the cold lockers, coming back with a basket of paper-wrapped food packages. "Here. Go. This won't be the only one of these I'll be fixing today."

Jakkin took the bowl in one hand, the basket in the other, and went out into the common room. He drank the *takk* as quickly as he could, letting the hot, thick liquid sear a trail down his throat. Then, rinsing out the bowl and spoon, he thrust them into the basket, covering them with one of the food bundles. If anyone asked, he would say . . . he could not think of what he would say.

The alarm bell rang loudly and Jakkin jumped. He could hear the sounds of bonders waking on both sides of the house.

Hoisting the basket onto his back and adjusting

the leather straps to fit his shoulders, he pushed open the heavy door and went out into the daylight.

As he left, Kkarina's voice echoed again in his thoughts: "Most men, after their first roundup . . ." *Most men.* Was the passage from boy to man really that easy? And was it always built upon lies?

Then, pushing the thought away, he bent his head and trudged off down the road as if he were going into town.

The dragon must have sensed his coming, for it was out of the shelter and waiting for him. It had only shreds of eggskin still clinging to its body, a strange patchwork of dull brown and yellow. Jakkin had a moment of disappointment. Dull brown. He had thought it was going to be a red. Browns were usually solid fighters, aggressive but without much imagination. Reds, on the other hand . . . he beat down the thought. Perhaps it might still change color. Hadn't he heard that *color fast does not last,* meaning a dragon's true color often did not show early. He could still hope.

He shifted his pack on his back and the coins in his bag clinked together.

At the sound, the dragon lifted its oversized wings. They still had a crumpled appearance and the effort of moving them seemed to tire the little lizard. It settled down again on its stomach and waited, head on front claws, for Jakkin to come nearer.

Jakkin smiled at the dragon and thought at it, "The morning becomes thee, my wonder worm."

The dragon's muted rainbow signature ran through Jakkin's head once more, as clear and identifying as if it were a mark on paper.

Jakkin knelt for a moment by the dragon's side and scratched it behind the ears and then down its long neck. The hatchling raised its back up, arching under his hand.

"Not yet, thou beauty," he said. He stood and walked into the shelter, where he shrugged out of the basket, unpacking the bowl and bone-handled knife. "First we must feed thee. Come on."

The dragon followed confidently at his heels as he walked to the weed and wort patch. In the direct sun, the leaves were all open as if turning every vein to catch the light. At the head of the patch, the dragon halted, digging its claws into the sand. It stood still, watching the movement of the wind through the stalks.

Jakkin was about to enter the patch, and stopped himself. This was the time, he thought suddenly, for the dragon's first lesson. He turned and faced it and held his hands towards it, palms up. "Good *stand*," he said, and then thought at it as well. "*Stand* still, thou mighty fighter. *Stand*."

He repeated the hand signals again and the spoken words, all the while thinking the sentence.

The dragon cocked its head to one side as if considering, but remained in the clawed-in stance.

Jakkin watched it carefully. After a minute, he could see it tiring, one leg beginning to waver. "Good *stand*," he thought at it one more time and went over and hugged it to him, rubbing it under the chin. "Thou mighty young snatchling. Thou great worm."

The dragon's tongue wrapped around his little finger and licked.

"Now for some food," Jakkin said. He walked back into the patch, careful not to touch the red stalks, which were still hotter than was comfortable, nor brush against the seed pods, which until they were covered with a gray film could give a bad burn. He plucked a handful of leaves and went back to the shelter, where he got out the bowl and knife.

Sitting down, feet in the stream, Jakkin cut the leaves, piercing the veins with the knife. Then he crushed the leaves with the bone handle. Before long, he had a half a bowl of juice.

"Here, eat this," he called to the snatchling, who was pouncing on shadows thrown by the kkhan reeds at the end of the pool.

The dragon looked over at his voice, but did not move.

"Come," said Jakkin, again, holding the bowl down so the dragon could see it.

The snatchling put its head to one side and lashed its ridged tail.

Jakkin thought at the dragon, "Come, thou hungry worm. Come." The dragon trotted over to him.

"So, thou needest an official invitation," said Jakkin, laughing as the dragon settled on its haunches and opened its mouth. He spooned the juice onto its tongue, missing whenever the dragon moved its head. Soon the two of them were covered with the dark maroon juice.

"Aw, fewmets," Jakkin said when the bowl was finished. "Look at this mess." Quickly he stripped off his clothes and washed the shirt and pants in the warm stream. His bag, too, was spattered with spots as dark as blood. He tried to rinse it as best he could, bending over the stream. As he was bent over, unbalanced, he felt a sharp nudge from behind, strong enough to thrust him forward. He tumbled head first into the water, went under, and came up spluttering to find the dragon in a hind-foot rise, its wings braced on the ground behind. It raked at the air with its soft claws. Jakkin could feel a rainbow laugh forming in his mind.

His moment of anger dissolved. The dragonling was so comical and fierce at once, he started to laugh instead. Then he realized what it was doing, and thought at it, "*Steady. Steady.*" Then, when he saw the dragon begin to falter, he cried out, "Good. Now."

The dragon lifted its overlarge wings and leaped into the river, landing next to him with a tremendous splash.

Jakkin laughed and splashed back.

At last they climbed out of the river together and flopped onto the sand. The sun on his back and shoulders and legs felt good. Jakkin lay on his stomach and thought about the dragon and about the possible fights ahead. "It will not be easy, little one," he said. "There is much I do not know. I was too young to learn much from my father. I am not old enough yet to be apprenticed to a trainer. And watching badly trained dragons in the Pits only teaches bad habits—I heard Master Sarkkhan say that once. He was talking to Likkarn, but I over-heard him. Master Sarkkhan said there were only two ways to learn about dragons—from a good trainer or from a good dragon. Likkarn *is* a good trainer, even if he is an awful weeder. But he hates me, I know. He would never take me on, even though he knows I am the best of the bonders with dragons. Maybe I should try to smile and be nice to him, like Errikkin. Only that's Errikkin's way, not mine. Or I could run away from dragons entirely, like Slakk. Only how can I? Dragons are my life. If Likkarn will not teach me, *I will fill my bag myself.*"

Jakkin sat up and stared at the hatchling. "If I can not learn from a good trainer, then I will learn it all from thee, who comes from a line of fighters, great fighters, from Heart O'Mine out of Heart Safe by Blood Type. Blood Brother was thy father and he was my special charge. And what I learn from thee, I will teach thee back. Together, heart of my heart, blood of my blood, we will be unbeatable. In time. In time." He lay back down and crooned the last words over and over and soon put the both of them to sleep.

Jakkin woke when the sun was high overhead. The dragon was standing guard beside him. He plucked some more leaves from the stalk and crushed out the juices, and only then took out his own lunch. It consisted of great hunks of brown bread spread liberally with the jellied protein that Kkarina had made, and a bottle of cold juice. There was cake for dessert.

Jakkin lay on his side eating and watched as the dragon ripped off the last shreds of its eggskin with its claws.

The claws were not as soft as they had been the day before, but were halfway between brittle and hard, and a strange yellow. They looked like the jingle shells found in Sukker's Marsh.

Jakkin loosened one particularly difficult piece of skin up behind the snatchling's hackle, and the dragon rewarded him by licking his hand with its tongue.

"Thy tongue is getting rougher each day," Jakkin commented. "Soon I will not find thy thanks such a pleasure." He remembered, suddenly, how Blood Brother had tried to groom him in the baths, lifting off skin with his rough tongue. And he remembered what had happened to Blood Brother after. He shuddered.

"No one shall do such a thing to thee, little wormling," Jakkin promised. "I will not allow it. Not ever."

The dragon turned its black eyes towards him and Jakkin felt as if he could see strange constellations being born in the endless night of its eyes. "Be thou ever my friend," he whispered.

The dragon answered him with a weak trickle of smoke through its nose slits. It was no more than a patch of light fog that for a moment obscured the dragon's mouth, then was gone. But that it *was* smoke, the first conjurings of the fire of a fighting dragon, Jakkin was sure.

He laughed, a loud eruption that startled the snatchling into backing up.

"No, no, thou fire breather, do it once again," said Jakkin, his voice alive with laughter. "A great pit dragon must breathe fire and smoke. I will give thee *more* juice to stoke thy furnace, for blisterweed and burnwort are the fuel for thy flames." He stood up and started for the weed patch, chattering at the dragon as he went. He continued his monologue down one row, looking for the healthiest, most mature plants, and up the next until he found the plant he wanted at the row's end.

He stopped abruptly. In the sand by the stalk, almost hidden by a leaf, was a single shoeprint. For a moment, Jakkin was ready to dismiss it. He himself had walked around the weed and wort patch in sandals. But the fact that there was only the tip of the print showing, as if the rest had been broomed away, puzzled him. He turned and ran back to the shelter and picked up his own sandals. Then, reluctantly, he walked back to the patch.

Kneeling down, he matched up his sandal with the print. The print was slightly smaller than his own.

Jakkin sat down in the sand to consider. "Bigfoot" was a name that the boys had often called him, for he had had enormous feet since he was very young. His mother, he remembered, used to say that someday he would grow into his feet, and he was growing still. But if his own sandal had not made that print, then someone else's had.

He tried to think who it might be. Had any of the boys said anything to make him think they knew of the oasis and the snatchling? He recalled them teasing him about Akki. Had Slakk been a little less sarcastic than usual? Or Errikkin a little more willing to please? Or any of the younger boys too familiar? Perhaps . . . yet he couldn't imagine them spying on him. He thought about the men, listing them in his mind. Balakk and his two were busy in the fields today. And Jo-Janekk was inventorying the store—or so he said. Frankkalin had been given the day as Bond-Off. Perhaps it had been Frankkalin. Or old Likkarn. What had he said before their march back? He had turned to Jakkin and spat out: "You'll have tomorrow as Bond-Off. I'm sure you'll *need* it, boy." At the time, Jakkin had thought old Likk-and-Spittle had meant he would need the time to recover from the bloody roundup. "But perhaps," Jakkin said aloud, "perhaps what Likkarn meant was that I would need the time for my dragon."

And Likkarn was a small man, small and wiry. He would have a smallish foot. Jakkin thought about it, and the more he thought, the more it all fit. Likkarn must have followed him out and watched as he and the dragon slept. It all fit except for one piece. Why, if Likkarn knew about the dragon, had he not reported it? What subtle motives did the old man have in keeping such a thing secret?

Jakkin got back on his knees and held his sandal over the print again. There was no mistake. His sandal *was* bigger, though not by much. Likkarn must have been there at some point, all right, watching. Watching and waiting. Jakkin looked around the oasis. It was no longer as bright, as clean, as beautiful. Likkarn's presence there cast a long shadow.

Reluctantly, Jakkin stood up and went to the shelter. He got dressed slowly, trying to think out his next steps. He would have to return to the Nursery and see if he could find out what Likkarn was up to. He was not afraid for himself. After all, what could Likkarn do to him? He was already a bond boy. Though his bag might be emptied, he could not be broken further. But Jakkin worried what the old weeder might do to the hatchling. If he could kill a great stud like Brother, how easy it would be for him to slaughter the defenseless dragonling. Kill it—or have it killed in the Stews.

Jakkin walked to the top of a dune escorted by the dragon. It ran around him, its legs having to work twice as fast to pull the weight of its oversized wings.

"Stay," Jakkin told it sharply. Then he knelt down by its side. "Stay, my beauty, till I come to thee again." He touched its nose.

The dragon seemed to understand. It crouched down, head on its front legs, wings folded back along its side.

Jakkin turned back only once to look at it, and by then it was fast asleep in the sand.

13

Jakkin scrambled onto the road once he was sure it was free of dust clouds, and turned to broom away his final steps. As he walked briskly towards the Nursery turn-off, the basket banging against his back, he tried again to sort out the possible meaning of the toeprint he had found. He was convinced it belonged to Likkarn. But what if it did not?

If it belonged to one of the young boys—Errik-kin or Slakk or Trikko, for example—he could probably buy the boy off with the coins from his bag. He jangled the bag, listening to the clank and nodding his head at how full it seemed.

If the footprint belonged to an older bonder, things would be more difficult. Perhaps he would have to offer a half-share in the dragon besides the gold. But he would make it clear that he, Jakkin, was to be the trainer. After all, the dragon already responded to him, already knew *his* mind.

But if it was Likkarn spying on him, then that would be the worst of all. The old man already blamed Jakkin for his latest de-bagging. He had made that quite clear.

Shifting the basket on his back, Jakkin turned onto the road lined with spikka trees that led to the Nursery. It was said that there were more spikka trees planted at Sarkkhan's Nursery than anywhere else on Austar. They were expensive, Jakkin knew, but they also helped make the ground fertile by drawing and holding water with their roots.

As Jakkin rounded the last turning, he saw the Nursery buildings spread out before him and, to the right, the red haze of the wort and weed patches. He let out an involuntary sigh and stopped. Except for a few snatches of memory, Sarkkhan's Nursery was all he knew. It was his home. And yet *not* his home, for when he had filled his bag, when he had trained his dragon and won his fights, he would leave and start the life of a master. On his own. Instinctively, his hand went first through his hair, then touched the dimple on his cheek, and at last rested on his bond bag, a habitual round he was not aware of.

He laughed out loud. "You can face drakk and dragons, but not your own waking dreams."

He started up again, determined not to fall prey to such fears, when a strange cackling sounded from behind the incubarn to his right. For a moment Jakkin did not recognize the noise. It was a combination of a hen chuckle and the frantic peep-peeping of hatchlings. Then he remembered. Today was the day of the first airing, when the hens and their broods were let out of the barn into the corral.

Jakkin took off the basket and set it by the side of the barn, where he would pick it up later. He loved to watch the first airing. There was nothing funnier than the rush of hatchlings as they ran about, watched over by the mother dragons and the bond boys.

The henyard was an open corral surrounded by a fence of planed spikka wood. A full-grown hen could easily step over or fly across the man-made border. But the mother dragons would not leave their broods, and the hatchlings would not be able to make more than a few wing-hops for several months yet. So they all stayed inside the enclosing arms of the fence. The hens crouched down like great stone statues, keeping their fathomless black eyes on the antics of the young. And bond boys scattered at intervals on the fence top made sure no injuries occurred, using long prod-sticks to separate overeager hatchlings, who were already establishing a pecking order that would last the rest of their brood lives.

Jakkin climbed up the fence and, holding on, peered over the top. He scanned the broods quickly. They were all out of their eggskins, the hens having helped remove the last patches. Jakkin knew that the bond girls had already collected the pieces of eggskin and begun the long task of sewing them together for clothes and coverlets and the hundred other items the soft, stretchable fragments could be used for. Jakkin looked in particular for the crippled hatchling in Heart O'Mine's brood, but he could not find it. It had probably already been culled. There were one or two runts that would be culled soon as well: a nearly white one cowered by the barn gate, smaller than the rest by half, and a finely spotted yellow weakling lay covered with dust by the foot of its mother, Heart to Heart. There was little doubt those two hatchlings would be early culls.

Jakkin sighed. He hated the thought of the culling, when the weakest dragon hatchlings were taken from their hens, squealing and peeping, and thrown into the truck bound for the Stews. He knew it had to be done, that such dragons would die before year's end anyway, stepped on or pecked into a stupor by their broodmates. If they were allowed to live long enough to stud or bear young, the resulting hatchlings would be even weaker than their parents. Jakkin knew all this, but it didn't make the terrible cries in the culling trucks any easier to bear.

He compared the hatchlings in the yard to his own dragon, and they all suffered by the comparison. These young dragons were spotted and marked with splotches of color. Except for one all-orange hatchling, one deep mustard-colored, and two gray-browns with yellow paws, there was not a dark red in the lot. His dragon, with its dull brown skin, had the best markings of them all. Of course, he reminded himself, color was not the only clue to a dragon's worth. And first color was not last. But he could not stop himself from smiling when he thought of his own dragon, as he had last seen it, a brown mound asleep on the sand.

Some of the hatchlings began to give mock battle, prancing around their hens and stepping on one another's dragging wings. The all-orange dragonling seemed the most ferocious, and it already could trickle straggles of fog from its nose slits when approaching an enemy. But it was the deep mustard dragon that had the best control of its oversized wings. It could hover for several heartbeats above the ground, confounding its brood-mates.

The lethargic hens occasionally stuck out their massive paws to separate two fighters when the going got too rough and the agonized peeping of a loser become too harsh on the ear. More often it was the bond boys who did the separating with the prod-sticks. In the end, only the orange, the yellow, and one of the gray-brown hatchlings were awake, pawing at the hens' tails while their brothers and sisters curled up under the hens' outspread wings to sleep.

Jakkin felt an elbow in his side and, turning his head, came face to face with Errikkin. "Back so soon?"

Jakkin nodded.

"I thought you might want the whole day off. Considering . . ."

"Considering?" Involuntarily, Jakkin looked down to check Errikkin's shoes. He was barefoot, one leg stuck through the gap in the fence.

"Considering . . . you know." Errikkin grinned and punched Jakkin's bag.

"Hey," called Slakk across the yard, his voice disturbing several of the sleeping hatchlings who stirred next to their hens. "Empty your bag again?"

"Oh, considering," mumbled Jakkin. They were talking about Akki. They thought he had spent the day with her. He was suddenly sure that neither of the two of them had been spying on him. Flushing with guilt, he climbed down from the fence and started to walk back to the bondhouse to get his basket.

"Wait," said Errikkin, "don't go yet. I have

something to ask you. I know you'll probably be the first of us to fill your bag and . . ." Errikkin stumbled over his words.

Jakkin was cold; his words came out in icy formality. "What makes you say that?"

Errikkin did not seem to notice his coolness. "You got extra gold for the roundup and now that everyone knows you're almost a man, you'll probably have other extras as well. It's only natural."

"Oh." Jakkin felt ashamed. He had thought again, for a moment, that Errikkin had been the spy. In a rush of companionship compounded in equal parts of relief and chagrin, he put his arm over Errikkin's shoulder. "Ask away, you baggy bonder. Ask—and it shall be given unto you."

Errikkin flushed. "Well, I was wondering. When you become a master, I'll still be in bond. I can't seem to save anything. I mean, I love the Stews. And the Pits." Errikkin's hands went up in mock dismay. "And if you have extra gold and all. Well, I mean, would you consider buying *my* bag? I'd rather work for you than old Sarkkhan. I mean, not that he's a bad master. It's just that I don't really *know* him. He's never here. And I do know you. And . . ." Errikkin smiled and shrugged.

Jakkin was stunned. Slowly he pulled his arm away from Errikkin and looked at the ground.

"Fewmets," said Errikkin. "I hope I didn't say anything to make you mad."

Jakkin looked up again and said, as much to Errikkin as himself, "I never considered. I never considered — " he began. "I mean, I never thought that once I was a master, it meant I could own bonders. I don't think I want that. I don't think I want that at all."

"Well, what did you think being a master meant?" asked Errikkin, incredulously.

"I thought it meant, well, being free. And doing *what* you wanted *when* you wanted. Like sleeping late. Or like training your own dragon. Or . . ."

Slakk, coming up behind them, overheard only part of the conversation and interrupted. "And how could any of us train a dragon on our own, lest it's a feral? And *you* should know the results of that piece of folly better than any of us. Didn't your father get gaffed by a feral yellow in the sands? I'd rather be a live bonder than a dead master, any day."

"You're going to be a dead bonder if you don't get back up on that fence," came a voice behind them. It was Likkarn, his eyes red with weed tears. "You, too, Jakk-boy. If you're here, your Bond-Off is over. Keep an eye on those hatchlings, or by the time I'm through with you, you'll stink as bad as a drakk." He jabbed a prod-stick at them.

The boys went back to the fence, but Jakkin couldn't stop thinking about all that had been said. It was only at dinner, after the broods had been herded back into the barn, that he realized he hadn't tried to match up the shoeprints with any of the bonders' feet. In fact, except for one quick peek at Errikkin's bare feet, he hadn't even looked. He would have to find out who had been spying—and quickly.

14

All the way back to the oasis that evening, Jakkin tried to sort things out. Then it occurred to him that returning to the bondhouse late at night afforded him the greatest of opportunities. He would simply take off his sandals before entering the sleep room and quietly match up his shoes against the others. The sleeping bonders would have their sandals neatly lined up by their beds. If he was quick enough, and silent, he could know in minutes who the possible suspects were. Except for Likkarn and Jo-Janekk, who had single rooms. He would have to think of another method for them.

Jakkin was so deep in thought, he almost tripped over the brown mound of dragon waiting for him.

"Fewmets, you nearly killed me," he complained. But the use of the word "you" confused the little dragon, and it sent tendrils of color questing into his mind.

Immediately contrite, Jakkin knelt down by the dragon and cradled it to him. "I'm sorry, thou mighty one." The snatchling nuzzled his bond bag and licked him under the chin. Then it butted him in the chest, and the force of its blow knocked him over.

"Is that how thou treats a friend?" Jakkin asked, pretending anger. But the dragon could hear the laugh in his mind over the false anger of his words, and it blew several small strands of smoke at him. Then it turned and trotted across the dune towards the weed and wort patch.

Jakkin followed. "Art hungry again, thou bag of lard? I shall go through this patch of weed too quickly if thou canst not control thyself." He laughed out loud both at his own awkward use of *thou* and at the dragonling who waited, jaws wide, by the patch.

Quickly Jakkin stripped the largest leaves from two stalks, pleased to see new buds growing from the stalks he had plucked earlier. Bonders said *springtime is sprout time,* meaning dragons and weeds both grew incredibly fast in the spring. And watching his own snatchling, now as high as his thigh, Jakkin could believe it. The little dragon followed him closely back to the shelter, where Jakkin got out the bowl and the bone knife.

Sitting in the sand, Jakkin began the work of crushing the leaf veins, with the dragon snuggled, mouth open, by his elbow. Jakkin had to push the hatchling away. "Move, thou wonder worm, otherwise I cannot get thy dinner ready." The dragon moved inches away, then settled down again, nose in the sand. Stretched out, the dragon was as long from tip to tail as Jakkin was high. Its wings, which that afternoon had still looked crumpled and weak, were already beginning to take on the rubbery sheen of maturity. In the fading sunlight, the dragon's skin was a mud-brown color, but when Jakkin squinted his eyes and took a closer look, he could detect a reddish glow beneath. Jakkin thought: another boy seeing that ugly brown skin might have taken the snatchling to the Stews right away. It would mean a few coins. Maybe even more than a few. The younger the dragon, the more coins. *The meat is sweeter nearer the egg,* as the stewards like to say. And besides, training a fighter was sure to be a long, uncertain process, a year at least till a dragon's first fight.

Suddenly the enormity of what he had done by snatching the dragon was borne down on him. A year. A year of sneaking out by himself and hiding the dragon in the sands. A year of training it in secret. A year . . . but what was a year to a bonder? Just never-ending days of work. In the Nursery the seasons were struck off in threes: the season of stud, the season of eggs and hatchlings, the season of training the new fighters and selling the rest. And Jakkin's part of the year was only dust and fewmets, fewmets and dust. But this year, the year of Jakkin's dragon, things would be different. He finished crushing the juice out of the leaves and poured some of it into the dragon's mouth. The snatchling lapped it eagerly, and waited for the rest. Around its muzzle, drops of the red liquid still glistened.

"See that thou turneth that color all over," said Jakkin sternly, drizzling the rest into the dragon's open maw.

The hatchling's tongue licked away the last of the juice, and its tail twitched in reply.

Later they paddled together in the warm spring, watching the sun go below the horizon. The sky seemed stained with blood. As he floated on his back in the spring, the bond bag heavy on his chest, Jakkin felt surprisingly at peace. He closed his eyes and let the light rainbows of the dragon's mind float by his closed lids. Mauve and pink and a color slightly paler than eggskin arced across the dreamscape. It was an unruffled reflection of the little dragon's world.

Suddenly the rainbows broke apart in a fever of tiny slashing red streaks and Jakkin heard a screaming hiss. He opened his eyes and automatically clutched the bond bag with his right hand. A dark shadow was crossing the red-drenched sky, and Jakkin saw eight feet of outstretched wings and talons fixed for battle. It was a male drakk. The water of the spring mirrored the blood color of the sky. The dragon was nowhere to be seen.

Above the spring the drakk began circling, catching the currents of air and dipping first one wing and then the other. Its body sensors picked up the scent of dragon. But it could not trace the dragon smell on water; what it caught was the odor of the hatchling that still clung to the sand and the reeds.

"Where art thou, beauty?" Jakkin called to the dragon, desperately afraid.

In answer, down by the kkhan reeds, from under the water, an earth-colored mound rose up, shaking itself furiously. The hatchling had sensed the attack and had escaped underwater, where the drakk could not find it.

"Stay in the water," Jakkin thought at the hatchling, wondering if, in its fear, the young dragon would even hear him. "Stay *under* the water, my wonder worm." Then he scrabbled onto the bank and ran, crouching over, to the shelter. He knew that any minute the drakk might make a slashing run at him. Without his clothes he had no defense at all. But the drakk, intent on the dragonling below, paid him no mind.

Frantically he dressed in his shirt and short bonder's pants, which would afford him only slight protection. On the floor of the shelter lay his old shirt, the one he had left for his snatchling. It smelled strongly of dragon. He put it on. Two layers were surely better than one. He picked up the bowl and the bone-handled knife. Then, taking a deep breath, he plunged back outside.

The circling drakk cast continually for the scent of its prey. Suddenly the dragon smell was strong again, emerging from the shelter. The drakk took aim at the smell, trying to distinguish the unfamiliar outline with its nearsighted eyes. It swept its wings back along its sides, cutting off the sensors, and dove.

Jakkin heard the cleaving of air above him and looked up just in time. He raised the wooden bowl as a shield. The rush of the drakk's attack knocked him down and its wings scraped across his face, but the thick bowl blunted the drakk's first charge, breaking off one of the talon nails.

Hissing furiously, the drakk winged away, banked sharply, and turned back for a second run.

Jakkin planted himself firmly in the sand, knife raised, and waited.

The drakk dove again but pulled up short. Standing up straight, Jakkin's outline was nothing like a dragon's. The confused drakk veered away at the last moment, but not before Jakkin's knife had sliced into its wingtip. Hissing in pain, the drakk charged again, heedless of the lies its eyes told. It raked the air above Jakkin's head with its razor talons.

Jakkin lifted his arm and plunged the knife up-

ward. The blade slid through the drakk's feathers
and cut into the air. The drakk's talon found his
wrist and left a cruel gash in it along the inner
arm, nearly to the elbow crease. If the one nail on
the talon had not just been broken, it would have
taken his hand off at the wrist.

Jakkin screamed in pain and fell to the ground
as the drakk wheeled back above the treeline. His
involuntary cry called the dragon out of the
water, and it ran to him, its tail lashing in dismay.

"Go back," Jakkin shouted. "To the water. Go
back." But the little dragon stood by his side and
urged him up with its nose.

Jakkin stood unsteadily, dizzy with pain, just as
the drakk started down again. He leaned against
the dragon, trying at once to shield it and to use it
as a support. He held the knife in his other hand
and waited. He knew that he would have only one
more chance at the horror, and he knew he dared
not fail.

The drakk dove. Its hissing preceded it and its
snaky head was as straight as a spear. It counted
on the hypnotic effect of its milky eyes to keep its
prey still.

Jakkin thought at his dragon: "Do not look
straight on it. Look to one side. And when I move,
move away from me. But not till I cry it." Only
the faintest wisp of color came back in reply, and
Jakkin prayed that the hatchling understood.

He could feel his jaw tighten and a sickness

compounded of pain and fear growing in his belly. What he had felt on the roundup was nothing compared to this. And he knew that if he and the dragon died out in the sands, they might never be found. He remembered his mother crying over his father's bloody corpse. No one would cry over his.

The diving drakk seemed to hang in the air, unmoving, yet careening towards him at a speed too fast for reckoning. Jakkin stood still for moments, for hours, for eternities. Then at the last minute, he shoved the dragon one way, threw himself the other, screaming, "Move. Move, thou beauty."

The dragon shot away from him, and Jakkin planted both feet wide to steady himself. He held the knife overhead.

The drakk, torn between the dragon smells and the true and false dragon forms, broke its dive for an instant, as if to veer off. In that instant, Jakkin thrust the blade under and into the drakk's neck where it joined the body.

Hot, foul-smelling drakk blood poured out over Jakkin's sleeve, coating it with a greasy, purplish color. The odor made Jakkin gag, then gasp, then collapse. He never saw the drakk fall, but it landed heavily next to him, its talons opening and closing in its death throes. One nail caught on Jakkin's outer shirt and ripped it open from neck to hem.

Cautiously, the dragon trotted over to the drakk. It shook its head as if to rid its nose slits of the terrible smell, then, carefully, from behind, it shoved the drakk body with one foot as far from the shelter as it could. Then it went back to Jakkin and nudged him with its nose. When there was no response, the dragon lay down next to Jakkin and began, purposefully, to lick his bloody wrist and arm with its rough tongue. One swipe, two, three, and the wound was clean, though blood continued to seep. The dragon curled its body around the boy, but it did not sleep. Every now and then its tongue touched the edges of the wound as if, by licking, it could close them.

Jakkin came to once to a great sunburst of color in his head, then passed out again, his face half buried in the sand.

Jakkin woke in pain. There was a vise on one wrist and a burning ache along his other arm. And there was a horrible smell all around him that, combined with the constant pain, made him want to throw up. With an effort, he controlled his stomach. He moaned, almost experimentally, and there was a sudden cool hand on his forehead.

"Shhh. Hush. It's all right," a voice whispered in his ear. Recognizing the voice, he opened his eyes, expecting to see the white walls of the hospice and to find that he had been dreaming. He saw instead the dark, shadowy outline of the shelter nearby. He turned his head towards the voice and stared.

"You." He couldn't think for a moment. The awful smell confused him. "You . . ."

Akki smiled down at him, her dark hair falling over one eye. She brushed it back with her hand. "This is getting to be a habit," she said.

Suddenly it all fit together. The one person he had not suspected of spying on him.

"You have awfully large feet for a girl," he said, and pushed himself up to a sitting position, despite the pain. "Almost as big as mine."

She laughed. "That's funny, I think. What does it mean?"

"It means I found one of your footprints by the weed patch. One you neglected to broom away. Only I thought it was Likkarn's," Jakkin said, still surprised.

"I didn't think I missed any," she answered.

"Sloppy," he said, and laughed.

"I learned my bad habits from you," Akki said. "How do you think I found you in the first place?"

"That night you pulled me in out of the cold?"

"Yes. I got up extra early and broomed away your steps."

"And tracked them back at the same time," he said. There was admiration in his voice.

"Yes." She smiled again, acknowledging his admiration.

"I guess I have a lot to be grateful to you for," he said slowly, looking around casually. He hoped that in all her snooping she had never actually *seen* the dragon. Maybe she just thought he had built himself a retreat here, an oasis for his days of Bond-Off.

"It's outside," she said.

He shifted the weight off his aching arm and looked at his wrist, which was expertly bandaged. "The drakk?"

"What's left of the drakk. You nearly took the neck off its body," she said. "And with a blunt kitchen knife that's impressive."

This time Jakkin smiled. "Left-handed, too," he said, glad to be able to boast about something to her.

"And your dragon is still standing guard over the drakk's body. Kicking sand in its face every now and then. The sand seems to help keep the smell down." She wrinkled her nose. "It's still pretty awful, but the dragon keeps kicking. What a wonder worm."

"Oh." All his fears were contained in the one word. Akki heard it and looked at him slowly.

"I won't tell," she said. "I'll *never* tell."

Jakkin kept staring at the bandage on his wrist rather than look again at Akki. The bandage ma-

terial was unusual. He looked up and for the first
time realized that Akki was wearing his old shirt,
the one he had given the dragon. It had no buttons left and was tied up in front in a big knot.
Her bond bag showed. And a lot of her skin. He
looked away. Then he looked back shyly.

She seemed to guess his thoughts and gestured
towards herself. "This shirt was too dirty to put
around your wrist, so I tore my own up. Then I
used this. It was split up the front, from the hem
to the neck. The drakk got it, I guess. So I had to
tie it like this. It smells, though. And so do you."
She hesitated a moment and added, "And so do I."
She actually blushed under his stare.

His wrist suddenly throbbed, and he winced.

"The wound was clean," Akki went on, speaking
in the same amused voice she had used in the
hospice. "The dragon was licking it and it had
already started to heal over. There are lots of old
stories about that, though I had never seen it in
real life. That dragon tongues can heal, I mean.
Your other arm was burned a bit from the drakk's
blood, but the shirt helped. And the dragon had
kicked sand on it, too. That seemed to help as
well."

Jakkin grunted and got to his knees. He was
dizzy and started to tumble back. Akki was at his
side and helped him up. He wasn't sure he wanted
to have to lean on her, but he had no choice: it
was either lean or fall. He would rather have died

than fall in front of her, so he leaned. She was both soft and hard and they both blushed. This time she looked away first.

"I fed your dragon," she said.

"What?"

"Juice from the wort patch. Wouldn't you know, I burned myself on one of the stalks." She held up her hand but it was already too dark to see the burn clearly.

"We'd better get back to the bondhouse. The moons have both risen." She helped him stand and put her arm around his waist and under his arm. She came no higher than his shoulder.

"You must have *very* big feet for such a small girl," he said.

She laughed again. "I do."

They stopped a moment, and he called out loud to the dragon, "Take care, my mighty healer." He was unprepared for the great rising bursts of color that came into his head, reds and oranges, and shining golds. He stumbled and put his hand to his temples.

"What's wrong?"

"The dragon . . . my head . . ." He was confused for a moment. Then he realized that the colors filled him up—made him stronger, but did not threaten to overflow his mind. "Bank thy fires a bit," he thought at the dragon. The colors ebbed slightly. "That's better," he said out loud.

"You must be weak from blood loss," Akki said.

The dragon came over and nuzzled against his thigh, turning its black eyes on Akki for a moment. Then it walked over to her and licked her free hand.

"It likes you," said Jakkin, surprised at how jealous that made him feel.

"Only because I have been helping you," she said. But she tickled the dragon behind its ears, and the dragon began a gentle thrumming under her hands.

"Thou fickle worm," Jakkin thought at the dragon, but aloud he said, "Look, Akkhan has started down. We had better get back."

"Not without the drakk," Akki said.

"The drakk!"

"Listen: you stink, I stink. And it's not a smell that usually accompanies a boy and girl out at night together. If we bring the drakk back, they'll just think we were out pair-bonding and got set upon by that . . . that horror. Oh, I'll tell them quite a tale about how you saved me and . . ."

Jakkin interrupted. "But they'll know. Drakks don't attack humans."

Akki thought a minute, running her free hand through her hair. "But hadn't you been out with the hatchlings this afternoon?"

"Well, yes, but how did you know?"

"I know . . . a lot," she said. "We'll tell them we think the drakk smelled the hatchlings on you."

"And knew that I had had a hand in killing his mate and chicks," Jakkin finished.

"I don't know if drakk think that way," said Akki.

"Or think at all," added Jakkin. "But who can say? That baggy piece of waste attacked us and I fought it off. And you, being a nurse, nursed me." He was really enjoying the story.

"And we'll bring the stinking carcass home and be heroes." She smiled.

"Until someone asks where I got the knife."

Akki frowned. "Oh, that."

Jakkin nodded his head. "That."

"This will take a bit more thinking," said Akki.

Jakkin stood apart from her, feeling stronger. "We'd better think as we go."

"You take the drakk. If you can. I don't want to touch it. And the knife. I'll do the brooming," Akki said.

He went over to the sand-covered drakk, circling from the back and kicking it several times to be sure it was really dead. He looked at Akki in case she was laughing, but drakk were no laughing matter. The drakk did not move. He picked it up by its talons with his left hand and slung it over his shoulder. It must have weighed over five kilos and it still smelled. He hated the feel of it against his back. He wondered if he would ever get the stench out of his skin.

Akki followed behind, brooming their path. She used a long broomer with a collapsible handle. "See," she said brightly, "no bending."

"I never thought of that," Jakkin said ruefully. She seemed to think of a lot of things he had never considered. He wondered how many other things she knew about: brooms and hospices, dragons— and men. There had been talk about her at the Nursery, about her and Sarkkhan. Guesses, really. Nursery gossip. No one knew much about her for sure, though Slakk often supplied tidbits he swore were true. She had arrived at the Nursery about three years earlier, Jakkin seemed to remember. Someone said Sarkkhan had found her at a Baggery. Someone else had once suggested she was the doctor's girl. She seemed to go where she wanted and when she wanted, almost as if she were free. But she was a bonder; her bag said as much. Jakkin suddenly remembered her standing by his bed at the hospice and scripting something. If she could script, she could read. And if she could read, she was either free, or very close to someone free. The doctor. Or Master Sarkkhan. Yet the way she had been acting this evening didn't sound as if she were Sarkkhan's girl. She talked about a boy and girl out together. She had followed Jakkin's tracks. She had rescued *him*. She had promised not to tell. If she were a free man's mate, pair-bonding with someone, surely she wouldn't act that way. Or would she? It was a riddle, a puzzle that Jakkin could not answer.

They walked most of the way in silence. Jakkin even stopped thinking after a while, because walking and carrying the heavy drakk took most of his remaining strength.

Near the Nursery road, Akki spoke at last. "I still haven't thought of any way to explain the knife," she said.

"Nor have I."

But in the end, no one asked. There was a great fuss when they set the dead drakk on the bondhouse steps and the smell woke the other bonders and set the hen dragons roaring. Jakkin and Errikkin, accompanied by a complaining Slakk and a sleepy Trikko, were sent to bury the drakk beyond the compound. They finished just before Dark-After, and hurried back for showers.

Jakkin was allowed to sleep the morning away. He did not see Akki again until that night.

15

Dinner was a special occasion, the first party since the twenty-fifth anniversary of the Nursery's founding. In honor of the drakk killers, Kkarina had made an elaborate cake covered with a deep red frosting and a candied figure of a dead eggsucker, complete with caramelized eyes and a bone-handled kitchen knife rising out of its stomach.

Even Master Sarkkhan ate with the bonders. Just back from a successful trip to a Minor Pit, the Nursery owner sat with the older bonders and regaled them with stories of his early fights. Only Likkarn was absent. Rumor had it that he had cursed Sarkkhan to his face, calling him "gold master" and a "drakk dodger." Jakkin wondered if the old man had been smoking weed again or if he was really jealous of Jakkin's success.

"Let him sulk in his room," Jakkin thought to himself. But he suddenly felt sorry for the old man who had led them all so fearlessly against the drakk colony. Now that he no longer thought that Likkarn was spying on him, threatening his hatchling, Jakkin could afford to feel sympathy.

At the dinner's end, Jakkin was summoned to Sarkkhan's table, where the master, still in the red and gold suit he had worn to the Pit, presented him with a handful of gold. Jakkin had never been face-to-face with the Nursery owner before. The man was big, massive, with broad shoulders and large hands that were covered with red-gold hair. He had an expansive smile.

"Here," Sarkkhan said, his bushy red beard waggling as he spoke. "Your bag is not yet full. Fill it with the thanks of the Nursery. One dead drakk means many live dragons."

Jakkin took the gold and opened his bag with two fingers, never taking his eyes off Sarkkhan. He slid the coins into the pouch and heard them clink one after another: one, two, three, four, five. Then he murmured his embarrassed thanks.

"The thanks are entirely on our side, young Jakkin," said Sarkkhan. "I've had my eye on you for some time."

Jakkin wondered briefly what Sarkkhan meant by that. Then he managed to smile back and add, boldly, "Some thanks and coin belong to Akki as well," he said, appending the ritual words: "Her bag is not yet full."

Sarkkhan houghed through his nose like a disgruntled stud dragon. From the boys' table there came a giggle. Jakkin recognized Slakk's laugh.

Sarkkhan's eyes narrowed and his mouth grew thin, though it still smiled.

"She *was* there with me. She helped," Jakkin said.

"So I've heard," Sarkkhan replied. "We appreciate your fairness. As to paying her gold . . ."

Akki stood at the pair-bonders' table and called out loudly, "I do not fill my bag with Sarkkhan gold." Then she walked out of the room.

Jakkin watched her leave. He started to go after her, but Sarkkhan's hand on his arm stopped him.

"Let her go," the Nursery owner said. "She has a head harder than dragon bone, and Fool's Pride to match. Like her mother. Go back to your seat." It was not a suggestion but a command.

Jakkin sat down again between Errikin and Slakk and replayed the scene in his mind. It was all suggestion; it could be read many ways. Was Sarkkhan jealous? Was he angry? Or was he merely amused? The other boys chattered around him as they finished off extra helpings of the cake. Jakkin seemed to be in two places at once: running through the conversation with Sarkkhan once again and sitting next to the boys. As he heard Sarkkhan's voice saying "Fool's Pride," Trikko was eating a second slice of cake—Trikko, who usually seemed to exist on *takk* and water. Akki stood and left the room to Slakk's whining complaint.

"Couldn't you have left me some scrapings of icing?" asked Slakk.

"Have a heart," Errikkin said. "You've had three helpings already. Jakkin . . ."

Jakkin turned slowly and focused on Errikkin. "Yes?"

"Tell us again. How did you manage to kill it?"

Jakkin repeated the tale once again, but his mind was really wandering outside with Akki. He could hardly wait for dinner to be over to find her.

Akki was not in the bondhouse at all. Jakkin finally came upon her by the southwest corner of the building. She was sitting in the sand, her back against the wall. She was fiddling with her bond bag and looking out into the distance, beyond the copse of spikka trees where the first drakk had been killed.

"Akki," he said quietly, and slid down the wall to sit next to her.

She didn't bother looking at him, but let the bag fall against her chest. It didn't make a sound. "Leave me alone."

"But you didn't leave me alone when I needed it."

"He knows I won't take his gold. I've told him

so before. There is always a hidden price to pay. No man's gold will go into *my* bag." She placed her hand protectively over the leather pouch and spoke in a fierce undertone.

"Sarkkhan?" He found himself whispering back.

"That bullheaded, stone-prided . . . I hate him." Her voice was loud again, and hard.

Jakkin sat up on his knees and turned to face her. "Now, wait a minute," he said, putting his hands on her face and forcing her to look right at him. "The gold in your bag was my idea, not Master Sarkkhan's."

"*Master!*" She spat the word out.

"Yes, *Master* Sarkkhan. Until I am a master, he is mine. And yours."

"No man is my master," she said.

He was shocked into silence.

"No man's gold will fill my bag," she said, and jangled her bag at him. It was totally empty. He reached over and crumpled it in his hand. Not even a grave coin. He had never known any bonder without that single coin.

"My mother was a Baggery girl," she said. "She died at my birth. The other Bag Girls raised me. But when I was twelve and knew that I wanted to doctor—people and dragons—and not live a Bag Girl's life, I left. So here I work. And learn. I am only fifteen. I have years of learning ahead. But no man's gold will fill *my* bag."

"I see," Jakkin said, though he didn't really.

"Come on. Never mind me. Let's go see your little beauty," Akki said, brushing her hair from her face and giving a swipe at her eyes as well.

Jakkin pretended not to notice. He had a feeling she wouldn't want him to see that she had been crying.

"All right," he said at last, standing up. He was about to reach down and give her a hand, when she stood up without his help. "Do you have the broom?"

"Don't I always?" she asked.

He nodded, and they walked down the road, slightly apart, but not so far that Jakkin could not feel the warmth of her by his side.

The dragon was asleep in the shelter. It did not even wake when they entered. They sat down next to it, listening to its hissing snore and watching the rise and fall, rise and fall, of its mud-brown sides. Its wings twitched slightly as if it dreamed of flying.

"Look," Akki said, pointing to the tail, "there's red coming through. A berry red, I think."

Jakkin looked. There was a patch of red showing, like a halo around the tail's tip. "Red. But deeper than berry."

Akki moved closer and stared.

"You're right," she said. "It *is* deeper. It's the same color as your blood was on the sand."

"Are you sure?"

"Didn't I see enough of it yesterday?" she asked.

Jakkin nodded and held up his wrist. It was only lightly bandaged and no longer hurt. "Dragon's tongue and heart's blood," he said.

The dragon gave a long, slow yawn and woke, stretching its wings and scrabbling with its claws on the sand.

"Up, thou lazy worm," Jakkin said aloud.

"Do you always speak *thou* to your dragon?"

Jakkin nodded. "At least I try, though I get my thees and thous mixed up a lot. My father knew dragons and he said the best trainers always use *thou*. It's supposed to bring me closer to the dragon. It seems to work."

She thought about that a moment. "I expect that's true with people, too," she said.

"Should I call you *thee*?" he asked impulsively.

"I'm not sure either of us wants to be *that* close," she said, laughing. "Yet."

For some reason, her laughter hurt. He answered quickly, "Besides, which of us would be the dragon, and which the trainer?"

"Well, I have the claws for it," she said, holding up her hands. They were large, sturdy hands. "But you have the bone head."

"Funny, that's what Master Sarkkhan said about you," Jakkin retorted.

"He should know."

Jakkin wondered what she meant.

"Come on, show me what this worm can do.

Besides eat, sleep, and cover drakks with sand."
She got up and ran out of the shelter, and the
dragon followed her, nipping playfully at her
heels.

Jakkin stood and went outside. For a minute he
watched the two of them playing. As Akki moved,
her long, dark, hip-length hair swung around her
body. The dragon caught a hank of the hair and
pulled. She fell to the ground and the dragon
jumped on her, and they rolled over and over to
the edge of the spring.

"Look out!" Jakkin warned. But he was too late.
They fell in together and swam apart.

Jakkin kicked off his sandals and took off his
shirt, and leaped in after them, dousing them both
with more water. Akki splashed back with her
hands, and the dragon fanned the water with its
wings.

"Enough," Akki called at last and climbed up
the bank on her hands and knees.

Jakkin reached out, caught her ankle, and
dragged her down again. When she resurfaced he
said, "I was only able to do that because your feet
are so big."

The last part of the sentence was lost in coughing, as he swallowed a wave she pushed towards
him. When the coughing fit was over, he saw Akki
and the dragon stretched out on the sand, drying
in the warmth of the desert breeze. He climbed up
after them and lay down a little ways apart.

Akki turned on her side and leaned on one elbow, facing him. The sand clung to her clothes and bondbag. "Now show me what this dragon can do. After all, you *are* trying to train a fighter, aren't you?"

Jakkin called the dragon to him, and showed her its stance. He had to hold the young dragon in place, but once the snatchling got the idea, it stood waiting for his nod of release. Then came the hindfoot. And finally, on command, it blew a few weak, damp straggles of smoke.

"Not much yet," said Jakkin. "But we've got a year. And this mighty worm is already way ahead of its clutch mates. They've just had their first airing. It's already bonded with me, fought a drakk, hovered, and blown smoke. Quite a dragon, don't you think?"

"But you've never trained a dragon before," she began.

"Of course not."

"Or seen one trained?"

"My father worked with ferals in the sands," Jakkin said. "I think I remember something of that. And I've sneaked about some in the Nursery. Last year I watched Likkarn in a session. And I'll try this year as well."

"What about going to a fight?"

"Well, I heard Sarkkhan say once that the dragon itself is the best teacher. And I'll need my gold for food and stuff."

Akki nodded. "I'll get you a book. Can you read? You were born free."

He nodded. "Some."

"Good," she said. "Or else I would have taught you."

"You *can* read," he said, more a statement than a question.

She ignored it. "I've seen several books on training at the hospice and some in Sarkkhan's cottage. I think I can get them for you without anyone suspecting."

Jakkin did not ask her why she had been in Sarkkhan's house. Perhaps she had helped treat him for an illness. She seemed to know him well—and hate him, too. Maybe the Nursery rumors were true. After all, she had been brought up in a Baggery. And though she had left at twelve . . . well, some girls started early. Sarkkhan had no wife, and Akki was beautiful. Maybe not as beautiful as the girl in Kkarina's portrait, but . . .

"Let's feed this beastie and go back home," said Akki. "I'm tired. And wet."

"We'll dry," said Jakkin, happy that she had changed the subject. "Long before we reach the Nursery and our beds, we'll be dry."

They stripped the leaves from three stalks and pressed out the juices with their nails, for they no longer had the kitchen knife. Then they washed their hands in the warm spring and went back.

16

Akki was as good as her word, bringing him three books on training over the next few weeks and white trainer suits for them both. Jakkin did not ask her where she got everything, or what she had to do to get it all. He did not want to know— and she did not volunteer the information.

He read the books with painstaking slowness, sounding out some of the harder technical words. And Akki, the few times she came out to the oasis with him, gave him lessons in dragon anatomy.

"Here, in the haunch," she said, pointing to the dragon's upper leg, "the big bone inside is called humerus. And the bending bone is the carpus, like our wrist bone."

He recited all the bones after her; humerus, ulna, radius, carpus, pointing to his own body and then the dragon's body, marveling at all the similarities. He wanted to know everything about dragons, inside and out. He learned the scientific names of the dragon's five claws from one of the books: the large double claws were the lanceae, the back three were called unum, secundum, and tricept, strange other-worldly words which he had to chant in order to remember. Akki tested him on the scientific names, and then he demonstrated the week's lesson with the dragon to her in return.

But Akki was not there as often as Jakkin would have liked. Most evenings she would start off with him, sometimes even holding his hand as they left the bondhouse. Then, at the main road, she would suddenly shake her head and pull her hand away, as if the hand-holding had only been a show for the others. She would leave him to go east toward the oasis while she took off on a more northerly path toward the Narrakka River. She warned him not to follow her. He never did.

He never did, because the dragon needed him. Even when it had outgrown the drizzled juice and could graze on the leaves and stalks of the blisterweed and burnwort that he picked for it—even when it was chest high and then past his shoulder —he could feel it calling to him in his head. It was a siren call he could not resist.

As so the season of the eggs passed.

During the day Jakkin joined Slakk and Errikkin, Trikko and the rest in cleaning the stud barns and mud-bathing the cock dragons. Likkarn was absent more and more from the barns, off to the Pits, it was said, his differences with Sarkkhan patched up once again. Jakkin did not miss him.

A new song was going the rounds of the Nursery now, called "The Minor Minor Pits" about a dragon who lost all his fights but one, and that one with the greatest champion of the world. Jakkin adopted the song for the mudbaths, and found its haunting tune with the slow rises and falls of the melody line wonderfully soothing to the excitable males. Even Bloody Flag, who had been unmanageable quite often since his stallmate's death, seemed to calm down and thrumm when the song floated by him.

Dust and fewmets and mudbaths filled Jakkin's days, but at night he worked with his own dragon, teaching it the rudiments of fighting in the Pits. All those feints and passes and stands that a dragon does naturally Jakkin gave names to, and he taught the names to his worm. By the end of the egg season, when the days grew shorter and the nights became a pavane of moons across the sky, Jakkin's dragon could respond to his every thought. He put it through its paces two or three times a week: left claw pass, right, hindfoot rise, stand. And the little dragon obeyed and improved at every lesson.

By the season of training and selling, Jakkin's dragon was far ahead of the dragonlings at the Nursery. They were just being separated into fighters and culls. The topmost hatchlings in the pecking order, those who had shown an instinct for blood, were automatically chosen for training. The quieter, frightened dragons were chosen for the Stews, though an occasional beauty, one marked with attractive spots or streakings, was set aside. Often Baggery girls or the masters' wives enjoyed such as pets. Gelded or spayed, the beauty-dragons never grew more than shoulder high and were gentle creatures of tidy habits.

Culling Day was always a horror. Great trucks drove onto the Nursery grounds, painted with the blood-red logo of the Rokk Stews: a dragon silhouette with crossed knives beneath, and the single word *Quality* outlined in gold paint like an aura above the dragon head. The bonders' foul mood communicated itself to the dragons. The hens stomped back and forth on their great feet, heaving and rocking their weight from side to side. They houghed and groaned. The hatchlings were silent beneath their feet; even the top of the order shivered, cowering next to their mothers' tree-trunk legs. In the stud barn came the bellowing of the males as if some memory of their own hatchling days was triggered there.

The food then was predictably bad, for Kkarina always absented herself on Culling Day, leaving the bonders to sort out her verbal instructions on their own. Something always went terribly wrong in the kitchen without her: the meat would be spoiled or the *takk* would not boil or the stoves would not function properly.

Only old Likkarn seemed to enjoy the culling. He preceded it every year with a night of blister fury. Jo-Janekk's swollen left eye and a bruise on Balakk's cheek testified to Likkarn's blisterweed strength. It had taken four of them to put him to bed. In the morning they all followed his orders sullenly. He was a weeder—but he knew dragons. His fingers pointed to one hatchling after another, sorting, hesitating only once at a well-spotted orange which was assigned, at last, to the beauty group. Jakkin was secretly pleased that he had guessed all but that last correctly. His eye was as good as Likkarn's.

He also knew that all over Austar IV similar Culling Days were held. It was reasonable to select the best dragons for breeding. Once, so the books told him, the great Austar dragons had been on the edge of extinction and the first settlers had slowly brought them back. The Encyclopedia had a whole article on the dragons. They used to fight one another to the death, and it had taken men to train them—retrain them really—to their old instincts of fighting only until dominance was assured. But that didn't make Culling Day any easier to bear.

Jakkin wondered briefly why the culling had to be so violent, why the hens and hatchlings had to be subjected to such a hard separation. But he knew that the only way to choose the hatchlings properly was to see them all together. And there was no practical way to quiet the culls' terror. Stunning the hatchlings would ruin the tender young meat for the Stews and could disorder the beauty-dragons completely. Besides, as Jakkin knew full well, there were very few power cells for the extinguishers to be had. They were used sparingly, and only in life-and-death situations.

That night, out on the oasis, Jakkin sat with his dragon's head in his lap. He sang it all the old songs he knew and tried to think pleasure at it while he scratched behind its ears. But the darker side of Culling Day must have nuzzled through his thoughts, for the dragon pushed his hand aside, stood up, and trotted beyond the weed patch. He heard it snuffling as it went. Leaving it to its own thoughts, he returned to the Nursery early.

Two days later, the Nursery had settled down again, the hens starting the long process of weaning their remaining hatchlings. In the oasis, Jakkin had to do the same. He made himself stay away, going back every third or fourth night with dread, fearing to find that the dragon had died of starvation without him. Each time he returned, the dragon greeted him joyfully, larger by another handbreadth than the last visit, and the weed and wort patch full of signs of its browsing. Jakkin was torn between pleasure at his dragon's growth—it was now as tall as he was—and a lingering disappointment that the snatchling did not seem to have needed him during his absence. But his pride in the growing strength and ability of his dragon soon overshadowed everything.

It was on the last day of the training season that he taught it a move that was in none of the books. It was an accident, really. They had been playing, though Jakkin now had to play with the dragon much more carefully. It was a little higher than his head, and its legs were the width of half-grown spikka trees. The scales of its back and neck and tail were hard and shiny as new-minted coins. Only along the belly and where its legs met the firm trunk were the scales still butter-soft.

Jakkin had rolled on the ground, propelled by a light tap from the dragon's tail, and had ended up on its left wing. The wing's ribs were encased in the hard grayish skin that contrasted sharply with the dragon's dark red body. Only at the knobby part of the wings, where the rubbery skin stretched taut, was there a hint of red in the gray. Shakily Jakkin stood up on the dragon's wing, careful not to scrape or tear it.

The dragon turned its head slowly to look at him, its eyes black shrouds.

"See, mighty worm, if thou canst free thyself

of this encumbrance," said Jakkin, standing very still.

The dragon opened its mouth and yawned, then fluttered its free wing slowly.

Jakkin began to relax. "Nothing? Canst do nothing?" he taunted gently. He watched the fluttering free wing.

Suddenly the tail came around and swept him off the pinioned wing in a single fluid motion. Caught unaware, Jakkin tumbled backwards and rolled into the embrace of the dragon's left leg. For a full minute it would not let him go. He could feel its laughter in his head, great churning waves of blue and green.

"And that," said Jakkin when the dragon let him up at last, "*that* we will call the Great Upset." He dusted his clothes off with his hands. "I *let* you knock me down. A dragon in the Pits will not be so easily fooled." He had started to walk away when the dragon's tail came up behind him and pushed him into the sand once again.

Jakkin laughed and turned over on his back. "You win. You win," he said as the tail came down and nudged under his arm, where the dragon knew he was especially ticklish.

And then it was the season of stud.

The bonders were kept busy day and night, helping the studs to preen, leading them one at a time into the arena-sized courtyards where the chosen hen waited. As the humans watched, the dragon courtship began.

The female stood, seemingly uninterested, while the male paced around the yard, measuring it with his eye. Every once in a while, he stopped and sprayed the floor with the extended scent glands on the underside of his tail or breathed smoky gusts onto the sand. His hackles rose. The circling continued until the hen either curled into a ball, pretending to sleep—which indicated that she was uninterested in the male—or until she leapt several feet in the air, pumping her great wings and lifting her tail.

If she turned down the courting male's offers, the bonders would jump into the ring and take the deflated dragon away. Deflated was the word, Slakk commented once, as he led Bloody Flag out of the ring. The male dragon's scent gland hung as loose as a coinless bag and his hackles had returned to normal size.

But once a hen accepted the male, showing her preference by her leap above the ring, the male winged into the air after her. Then they both shot into the sky, above the roofless courtyard, the female screaming her challenge to the male, who followed always slightly behind. They rose screaming and spiraling above the Nursery, higher and higher until they were merely black, swirling specks in the sky.

An hour later, the frantic courting flight over, the two returned together, wingtip to wingtip, to the courtyard, where a moss-covered floor-pad had been rolled out by the bonders. There, in full view of the watchers, the cock dragon mounted and mated with the hen. Then they lay side by side for the rest of the night. The following morning, separated by mutual consent and the prodsticks of the bonders, the stud went back to his own stall, the female to the incubarn. Neither would be used again that season.

Jakkin only managed to get to the oasis one evening a week during the season of stud, for he was suddenly promoted to helping with the matings, under Likkarn's direct supervision. It was not an easy job. It also meant that he shared Bond-Off with Likkarn. Jakkin's one worry was that the old man would track him over the sands just for spite, to get even with him for every mistake—real and imagined—that Jakkin made in the mating courtyards. But each Bond-Off Likkarn disappeared first. After the third Bond-Off, Jakkin relaxed his guard. He guessed that Likkarn had found someplace away from the Nursery to spend the day smoking blisterweed, since each morning after Bond-Off Likkarn's eyes were a furious red.

It was on that third Bond-Off, as Jakkin and his dragon were lazing in the sand after a hard session of training, that Jakkin thought about the latest mating flight he had seen.

"Canst use thy wings yet?" he asked, picturing the wild mating spiral in his mind. "Canst thee do more than a hover?"

The dragon responded by pumping its wings strongly, stirring the sand and making little frothy eddies in the stream. Then, as Jakkin watched, the dragon began to rise. Its great wings pumped mightily and Jakkin could see the powerful breast muscles moving under the shield of skin. The dragon rose as high as the shelter roof; then two more pumps brought it above the treeline, where it hovered a minute. Suddenly it caught a current of air and rode off into the sea of sky.

Jakkin stood, one hand over his eyes, straining to follow the disappearing dragon. He bit his lip and touched his bag. Now that it knew what its wings were for, the dragon might never return. It might go feral, finding a colony of wild dragons out beyond the mountains. Loosing a feral—that had always been a possibility. And yet he hadn't believed it. Not with his dragon, not really.

In the Nursery only the mating dragons were ever allowed to fly. And since they were not ready for mating until the females were two years old, the males three and quite settled into Nursery routines, there was rarely a Nursery dragon that went feral. Only one that Jakkin could remember had ever gone from Sarkkhan's Nursery—a red-gold stud on its first mating flight, a stud named, appropriately, Blood's A Rover. It had happened when Jakkin had first helped in the barns. Likkarn had raged for days, and everyone had felt the back of his hand or the lash of his tongue.

For over an hour the sky was empty and Jakkin was near despair. And then the dragon was back, wheeling and diving and cresting the waves of air with the same buoyant grace it had ridden the stream. Finally it settled down, landing on the ground with an earth-shaking thump right next to Jakkin.

He looked at it with a great smile on his face. "There is none like thee," he said, moving to it and circling its neck with his arms. He put his cheek on its scaly jaw. "None."

He was rewarded with a cascade, a waterfall, a sunburst of color, and this time he did not ask it to mute its fiery show.

the
fighter

17

The year traveled straight across the season, but Jakkin saw only the wavy lines of progress that his dragon made. By year's end, the dragon towered above him, and it was hard to recall the little hatchling in its yellowish eggskin that had staggered around the oasis under the weight of its oversized wings. This yearling dragon was a beautiful dull red. Not the red of hollyberry or the red of the wild-flowering trillium that grew at the edge of Sukker's Marsh, but the deep red of life's blood spilt upon the sand. The nails on its foreclaws, which had been as brittle as jingle shells, were now hard—the lanceae were almost indestructible. Its eyes were two black shrouds. It had not roared yet. But Jakkin knew the roar would come, loud and full and fierce, when it was first blooded in the ring. The quality of that roar would start the betting rippling again through the crowd at the Pits, for they judged a fighter partly by the timbre of its voice.

Jakkin dreamed of the Pits at night, fretted about them by day. The closest Minor Pits—for a First Fighter could never start in a Major Pit; that was only for champions—was past Krakkow, the town that was fifteen kilometers from the Nursery. Jakkin had tried to ask seemingly innocent questions of the other bonders about the route to Krakkow and beyond, because Akki had never been to the Minor Pits there. But Likkarn had overheard one such conversation and had interrupted it as he passed by, asking, "Checking out the fighting dragons for some purpose, boy?" as if he knew something. So Jakkin had stopped asking anything. He had debated going one Bond-Off to the Minor Pits to check it out himself. But the trip by truck cost a coin, as did the entrance fee to the Pits, though Slakk said there were ways to sneak in. And he might have walked there and back in a long day, but he needed the Bond-Off to train and he had little enough gold left in his bag. Most had gone with Akki to buy more burnwort and blister-weed seeds. He never asked her how she got it, only thanked her when she handed him the precious paper packets of seeds.

He could have stolen what he needed from the Nursery stores. Just a handful of seeds seemed an insignificant thing. But he never even considered it, just as he never considered sneaking into the Pits. Taking an egg or a hatchling was acceptable thievery, the mark of a possible master. But taking supplies from a Nursery might condemn an older dragon to short rations in a bad year. It could even mean death to the Nursery worms. And sneaking into the Pits meant cutting into the most basic part of Austarian economy. Besides, if he was caught it was punishable by a prison term on another planet. Jakkin simply would not do such a thing.

One evening, while Jakkin was putting the red through its paces, Akki came slipping quietly through the weed and wort patch. The old shoots were mostly all grazed down, but the new crop, planted with the purchased seed, was sending smoky signals into the still air. Akki's passage moved the gray smoke away from the stalks, and some of the clouds clung to her dark hair, crowning it with fuzzy gray jewels. She tried to brush the stuff off her hair and bond bag with impatient hands.

"Akki," Jakkin cried out when he saw her, unable to disguise the pleasure in his voice. It had been many days since she had visited the oasis.

She grinned lopsidedly. "I've brought you a present."

"A present? For me? What?" He sounded like a child, and willed himself to stop chattering.

She opened her bond bag and reached into it, withdrawing some crumpled pieces of paper.

"Registration papers. For the Krakkow Minors," she said, holding them out to him.

"I don't understand," Jakkin began.

"I didn't think you would. You have to sign these papers in order to fight your dragon at the Pit. They don't just let *anyone* in, you know." She shook her head at him.

"But my father never . . ."

"Your father was training a feral," she reminded him. "And he never got far enough along with it to register it. Ever since—well, the constitution at least—there have been rules about this sort of thing."

Jakkin suddenly felt as crumpled as the paper. "I didn't realize. What would I have done?" He began half a dozen other sentences and finished none of them, mumbling half to himself and half to Akki.

"Never mind," said Akki. "I've gotten the papers all filled out. All you have to do is sign them with your mark."

"That's all?"

"That's all. I'll take the papers in and file them with the right people," Akki said. "And then, on the right day, you and the dragon will be there. At the Pits. *If* you think your dragon is ready."

"Ready?" Jakkin gestured at the dragon. "Just look." The yearling dragon was lying by the side

of the stream. It stretched out parallel to the
bright ribbon of water, its red contrasting with
the blue-white. In the moonlight, both the water
and the dragon scales shone equally. Slowly its
tail rose and fell, weaving little fantasies in the
air.

Akki nodded slowly. "Thou art a beauty, in
truth. In truth," she said, her voice free of its usual
mocking tone.

At her voice, the dragon stirred and looked
around at them.

"So," said Akki, turning back quickly to Jakkin.
"How do you propose to get the dragon there?
Walk along the main road with that great thing
galumphing at your side? Or sneak it under the
cover of darkness and get frozen during Dark-
After?"

Jakkin looked down at his feet. It had been a
question that had troubled him frequently and he
had put off thinking about it.

"Perhaps . . . I thought . . ." he began, then
finished with a rush. "That the dragon could carry
me."

"Look," said Akki, and she pulled him along by
the hand to where the dragon lay in the sand.
Then, as if giving a fairly stupid child a lesson in
spelling, she pointed: "The dragon's shoulders,
here and here, are too thin and smooth-scaled for
sitting. The hackles would be damaged by pres-
sure there. And if you tried to hold on there or

there," she touched the dragon along its long, sinuous back, "the slightest turn of its body would send those sharp-edged scales slicing into you at your most tender points."

Under the withering lecture, Jakkin held his shoulders rigid and fingered his bond bag with one hand. Akki was right. And the worst of it was, he had already figured that out for himself.

"It's been tried before, dragon riding," said Akki. "And the men who tried it had scars they would not even show the Bag girls." Her voice got hard. "The ones that lived."

"I was thinking more of a harness," he said quietly. "With a swing of some kind."

Akki was silent for a moment. "Hmmm. You know. It might just work. If . . . if you had more training time. And a dragon whose claws you didn't mind ruining while you practiced. But this, my boy, this dragon is a *fighter*."

"You don't need to remind me," said Jakkin, straightening up and walking away. Akki always made him feel two ways. He was happy to see her but he was angry at her long lecture, at her calling him a boy. He had already proven his manhood— fighting drakks, stealing and training a dragon. What more did *she* want, anyway? His anger communicated itself to the dragon, who blew a sudden hot breath at Akki's foot.

Akki caught up to Jakkin and touched his shoulder. "Then what are you going to do?"

Jakkin flinched from her touch and sat down suddenly in the sand, his head and arms on his knees. "I . . . don't . . . know." He said it with a finality that precluded pity.

Akki sat down opposite him, her toes touching his. She pushed his head up with the palm of one hand. "I do!" she said, and waited.

He looked at her but could not speak.

"I have . . . friends with a dragon truck," she almost whispered. "A big hauler."

"You said," Jakkin began, each word an accusation, "you said you would tell no one."

"I haven't. Yet."

"Then don't. *I fill my bag myself.*"

She heard her own voice echoed in his and nodded. "But what else can you do? Your fight is scheduled in three days." She held out the papers again.

"What?" He grabbed the papers and smoothed them out. Slowly he read the print by the weak light of Akka.

AGREEMENT made this 127th day of Stud, 2507, between the management of the Krakkow Minor Pit and Jakkin Stewart of Sarkkhan's Nursery.

WITNESSETH

In consideration of the mutual covenants herein contained, the parties agree as follows . . .

"Where does it say that?" Jakkin asked, the words on the page a jumble. Some of the words he had never even *heard* before, much less spelled out.

"There," said Akki, her finger pointing halfway down the first page.

Jakkin looked. In between the words "Jakkin's Red" and "First Fight" was a date. "It *is* in three days," Jakkin said.

"It was the only opening," Akki explained. "The season is already booked up with dragons from all the major and minor nurseries. But in this one fight, a dragon dropped out, a promising Second Fighter. The dragon escaped somehow. Went feral. Its owners are wild themselves. They've even accused someone of pirating, of setting the dragon free. Anyway, I was able to get the place for you. Don't ask how. It wasn't easy. But it's your only chance at Krakkow this season."

Jakkin looked up. He was about to thank her when he stopped, remembering her words of nearly a year ago. "You once said to me that letting another person fill your bag meant that there would be a hidden price to pay."

Akki smiled crookedly at him. "What a memory you have," she said. He felt, oddly, like a small child being praised. "It all depends whether you think that what you are getting is worth the price, I guess."

Jakkin looked over at his dragon. "A First Fight. In three days," he said. "It's worth it." He hesitated. "It's worth anything."

"Are you ready?"

"The question is really whether the dragon is ready." Jakkin answered, wondering why she shook her head at his reply.

At his voice, the dragon looked up and shot a single flame at them, neatly parting the two.

"Ready," said Akki, and she began to laugh.

18

Akki's planning was perfect. Jakkin's Bond-Off coincided with the day of the fight. He was dressed and off to the oasis as the cold of Dark-After was still receding, a paper sack containing a slab of meat between two slices of bread inside his shirt. It was left over from the evening's meal. He had been too excited to eat it, almost too excited to sleep.

At the oasis he polished the red's scales from tip of tail to nostril slits. The first polishing was in the stream, where he made a mudbath of the sand, stirring up the stream bed until the water ran brown. The second was on shore, where he dried the dragon with an extra shirt Akki had provided.

Well before the full sunrise, Jakkin was walking out across the desert, the dragon trotting docilely at his heels, heading first north and then west, well away from the Nursery, to a ford in the Narrakka River. He had promised to meet Akki and her friend there.

The truck was waiting. He recognized it from Akki's description, but caution, an old habit, claimed him. He warned the dragon: "Drop. Stay." The dragon squatted down on its haunches, waiting.

Jakkin went ahead on his own, conscious of the great silent mound of dragon behind him. He was ready, at an instant's notice, to send the dragon a silent command that would have it winging into the air, past the oasis, to the far mountains, where it could live free. He walked up to the truck and knocked tentatively on the door.

A man looked out of the cab. His eyes were a calculating blue, his moustache full, and his skin neatly tailored over his bones. "Jakkin, is it?" he asked.

Jakkin nodded and, hearing steps behind him, turned quickly.

"Hello," Akki said. "This is Ardru." She pointed to the man in the truck, who opened the cab door and stepped down.

He was a bit taller than Jakkin, with an old scar that ran from the corner of his right eye to his sideburns. It gave him a piratical look. Ardru put out his hand. "I'm always happy to help Akki's friends," he said. His voice was low and he spoke the language so precisely that Jakkin could hear each syllable. Ardru smiled. "She appears to have a lot of friends."

Jakkin hesitated a moment. Ardru's name—if it was his whole name—lacked the *double k* that would identify him as a bonder, a son of bonders, a grandson of bonders. Only those whose ancestors had been the original masters—and there were very few left—had names free of the jailer's brand, *kk*. Jakkin had never met one before. He touched his bond bag with two fingers while he decided, then suddenly he put out his hand. Ardru's grasp was cool and firm. Jakkin thought at his dragon, "Fly to me, now, thou First Fighter."

The air hummed with the sound of dragon wings and the sand stirred around the wheels of the truck as the red flew in and hovered. Then it turned tail down and, using the tail as a rudder, settled slowly to earth, backwinging carefully.

"Thou art an impressive worm," said Ardru aloud, fearlessly walking up to the dragon. He held out his hand for the dragon to sniff. Satisfied, the dragon houghed once and sat down.

Jakkin, too, was satisfied. The dragon filled his head with cool green and beige landscapes.

Ardru unzipped the back doors of the truck and gestured to Jakkin. Jakkin climbed into the cavernous canvas-and-frame body of the truck, checking the insides for anything sharp that might injure the dragon. When he found none, he coaxed the red in after him. The red responded at once, climbing into the truck with an eagerness that matched Jakkin's own. The whole truck shook as the dragon settled down with its tail tucked around its feet and its nose on Jakkin's sandaled feet.

"Come ride up front with us," said Akki, peering into the darkness.

"No," Jakkin replied. "The worm needs me here."

"It will do just fine without you," said Akki.

"The boy knows best, Akki," said Ardru, putting his hand on her arm.

The easy familiarity with Akki and the smooth way Ardru called him a boy angered Jakkin. He started forward, but the doors were zipped shut on his movement. And then everything was black. He could see nothing through the heavy dark canvas, but he could hear the dragon's tail pound a sudden warning tattoo as it read the anger in his mind.

The ride to the Pit was a series of thudding bumps and shimmies. Jakkin leaned against the dragon's side and tried not to absorb the shocks through his bottom, but by the trip's end he ached in every bone.

The sudden shuddering stop of the truck and the zigzag of light through the opening door seemed to happen simultaneously.

"Come on out. Hurry." It was Akki.

He got shakily to his feet and went to the door, his eyes drawn into thin slits to keep out the sun. Together Akki and Jakkin backed the dragon out of the truck.

"Where's your friend?" he asked as the red lumbered out and stretched.

"Standing watch," she answered.

Jakkin looked around. They were still in the desert, the tan truck disguised by the dunes. But ahead, about a kilometer away, he could see a large building squatting like a monstrous round beast on the sand.

"That's the Pit," said Akki, nodding at the horizon with her head. "We didn't want to dump you out there. We can't have anyone know we helped you. I would get into trouble—real trouble —at the Nursery. And Ardru—well, he has to remain anonymous in all this. Do you understand?"

"Then that's not his real name?" asked Jakkin.

"Real enough," Akki answered. "And *that's* all you need to know. In fact, you should probably forget all about him. If I had been able to drive, I never would have asked him to help."

"I'll never tell," Jakkin said, looking at her. "That was a promise you gave me once. Remember? Only I keep my promises."

"And if I had kept it completely, would you be here now?" she asked. "Or if I had not been the watcher, but Likkarn? Or Slakk? Or even Errik-kin?"

Jakkin said nothing.

"Oh, go on, Jakkin. I *have* kept my promise to you—in substance, if not in words. Go on. Besides, both of you could probably use the walk."

Feeling the tightness in his muscles echoing the tightness in his throat, Jakkin nodded. He did not trust himself to speak.

A piercing whistle recalled Akki to the truck's cab. Ardru came around from the other side.

"All is clear," he said to Jakkin as he climbed into the cab. "And boy . . ."

Jakkin looked up into the man's coolly assessing eyes. "Yes," he said, his voice hesitating between resentment and thanks.

"That is a mighty fighting dragon you have there. You must treat your dragon as you would a woman—with respect as well as love."

Before Jakkin could think of an answer, the truck had started with a muffled roar and pulled away, leaving great ruts in the sand.

Jakkin put his feet in the ruts and walked slowly along. When he looked behind, the dragon was following him docilely.

The Krakkow Minor Pit was a huge, round two-story building constructed between two small cities but within the jurisdiction of only one—Krakkow. Jakkin could see a great center bubble illuminated from within, which probably contained the Pit itself. He had been told that there were tiers of stands where bettors sat, and a series of stalls on the lower floors.

He checked the contract once again and the letter that Akki had given him. It told him nothing beyond the number of his fight—tenth draw—and the number of the stall to which "Jakkin's Red" was assigned. First Fighters usually had the master's name and color description as identification. Naming would be done later.

"Stall 24," he whispered over his shoulder to the dragon. In the early morning light, the dragon's red scales were lustrous even with their patina of road dust.

As they came nearer the Pit, there was an explosion of sounds and smells and the flash of colors as dragons were unloaded from trucks, pushed and chivvied through two wooden gates. Jakkin heard the high-pitched scream of an angry dragon and watched as a gigantic brown with a splash of yellow across its muzzle went into a hindfoot rise. It towered over the truck it had come in. A scattering of men with smaller dragons warned Jakkin to hold his red close.

"Steady, steady," he thought at it, but his own tenseness communicated itself to the dragon. It sent a series of lightning strokes jetting through his head.

The great brown was calmed at last by a man who struck it on the sensitive end of the nose with a prod-stick. The dragon slinked through the gate with several well-dressed men after it. Nearby an orange dragon shifted its weight back and forth and houghed its distress. The sound was picked up by others nearby.

Jakkin's dragon sat for a moment and looked around. Jakkin went back to it and stroked its muzzle, then scratched behind its ears. "There's weed and wort for you inside, my beauty," he said. "And then you can show them all what you can do. But come. Come. Calmly."

The dragon turned its black eyes on Jakkin and they stared at one another for a long time. Something very like a bridge formed in Jakkin's mind and he fancied that two colors, a primary red and a primary blue, met in the middle of it. Then the dragon stood and followed Jakkin across the hard-packed earth and through the gates, where a bored guard stamped the papers that Jakkin carried in his bag. The guard took a quick picture of the dragon, affixing it to a badge which he pinned onto Jakkin's shirt so carelessly that it fell off before Jakkin had taken two steps. Jakkin picked up the facs badge and pinned it back on himself.

The underpit stall number 24 was a solid wooden affair, and the foodbin was piled high with fresh stalks and leaves. The dragon munched happily on them while Jakkin took the meat and bread from inside his shirt. Even wrapped in brown paper, the meat drippings had spotted his clean shirtfront. Jakkin tried unsuccessfully to rub the spots out.

"Maybe," he mumbled to himself, "maybe they look like dragon blood." But what they smelled like, he knew, was sandwich. He had dressed carefully that morning, but now looked like a poor bonder. Shrugging the annoyance away, he settled down to grooming the red with a cloth he found on a hook in the stall.

Noises came through the wooden ceiling. Jakkin could hear the groans of the floor joists as bettors and onlookers crowded into their seats. A disembodied voice called the names of the dragons for the opening fight: "Sarkkhan's Heavy Heart and Nokkar's Gold Digger."

Sarkkhan, here at the Pit! And with a named dragon! Jakkin found himself suddenly aware of the loud drumroll of his own heartbeats. Why hadn't Akki warned him? She must have known. Why hadn't he found it out himself? Surely he could have asked Balakk or Jo-Janekk or any of the other older bonders. It was information that was easy to discover. But he had been so afraid of being discovered that he himself had discovered nothing. He cursed his own incompetence, his own inadequacies. He was a *boy*, indeed. And now he could only hope—hope that Sarkkhan would win and leave, or lose and leave. He did not know what he would do if the Master recognized the red.

Suddenly he laughed out loud. How *could* Master Sarkkhan recognize the red? He had never seen it. "Thou art mine," he whispered fiercely at the dragon. "*I* took thee and *I* raised thee and *I* trained thee." He attacked the dragon's scales with the cloth as if they were an enemy to be rubbed out. "And thy name is *Jakkin's* Red."

The dragon was too busy munching on the wort to reply.

Then the noises overhead changed. Jakkin could hear cheers and an occasional raucous call. He could not distinguish the words, but the intentions were clear. And above it all were the loud thumps and screeches and roars of the dragons as they battled for supremacy in the Pit.

A pattern developed, and Jakkin, still cleaning his own dragon, heard it and made it a part of his own respiration. In the reactions of the crowd he could hear attack and counterattack, feint and thrust. He could translate the dragon screams into passes and charges, the thuds into wingleaps and an occasional hindfoot rise. But he was unprepared for the sudden stillness at the fight's end, and when it came, he held his breath.

Then, floating into the silence, violating the peace, the mechanical voice called out: "Game to Heavy Heart."

Sarkkhan's worm had won the first draw. Jakkin

did not know whether that was good or bad. He bent down over the red's claws and polished the lancea of the right front foot with special care. He did not even notice when Sarkkhan's winner flowed through the dragonlock and went back into its stall.

19

Jakkin lost count after the sixth fight, but he could hear, overhead, the pit cleaners circling noisily, gobbling up old fewmets with their iron mouths. They spat out fresh sawdust and moved on. It generally took several minutes between fights, and the mechanical clanking of the cleaners was matched by the roars of the pit-wise dragons and the last-minute betting calls of their masters.

Jakkin's fingers reflected his nervousness. He simply could not keep them still. They picked off bits of dust and flicked at specks on the dragon's already gleaming scales. They polished and smoothed and polished again. For the moment the red dragon seemed impervious to first-fight jitters and arched up under Jakkin's hands.

The cleaners clanked out of the ring through

the mecho holes and Jakkin looked up. He ran his fingers through his hair and tried to swallow; then he touched the dimple on his cheek. Finally his hand found the bond bag and kneaded it several times for luck.

"Soon now," he promised the dragon in a hoarse whisper, his hand still on the bag. "Soon. We will show them a first fight they will remember."

The only sounds came from the dragon's jaws as it munched on the remaining stalks in its bin.

The disembodied voice announced the next fight. "Jakkin's Red, Mekkle's Bottle O'Rum."

Jakkin winced. He had overheard a little about Bottle O'Rum that morning when he had gone out once to find more wort leaves. (Burnwort stoked a dragon's internal fires and made its flame hotter in a fight.) The dragon masters and trainers did not chatter while they groomed their fighters, but the bettors did, and Jakkin had chanced upon a knot of them by a stall. There were three in the fancy coveralls that the Austarian free men at the Pits affected, and one offworlder, the first Jakkin had ever seen. He was wearing a sky-blue suit covered with gold braid. Jakkin had known him for a rocket jockey at once because of the planet name and number emblazoned on his pocket.

The bettors had said, among other things, that Mekkle's Bottle O'Rum was a light-colored orange male that favored its left side and had won three of its seven fights—the last three. It would never be great, the whispers had run, but it was good enough in the Minor Pits. Jakkin had stored that bit of information away in his head, along with a lot else.

And now, Jakkin thought miserably, he could use what he knew. Bottle O'Rum was a hard draw for a new dragon and possibly disastrous for a would-be dragon master. If Mekkle could afford to run his dragon for four losing fights, until it was pit-wise and old enough and strong enough to win, then he must own a Nursery. Jakkin, with a bag now almost empty of even its grave coin, had no such option.

Jakkin knew his red would be good in time, even great, given the luck of the draw. It had all the things a fighter was supposed to have: it listened well, it had heart, it did all that was asked of it. "And more," he whispered. "And more."

But the red was not a particularly large dragon and this was its first fight. Not only that, but it was unused to the company of other dragons. It was starting to get really nervous, rolling its eyes, houghing at loud noises. It had even begun to hackle when he had first brought it into the stall though he had been able to calm it quickly. It had never been in a ring, not even in a corral or training ring behind a barn. What chance would it have fighting a pit-wise three-time winner? The red had never been blooded or given roar. He had been crazy to think they had a chance.

Already, Jakkin supposed, the betting would be running way against the young red. He thought he could hear the murmur of new bets following the announcement of the fight. The odds would be so awful, he might never get a sponsor for a second match, even if the red showed well in the Pit. First fights were free, Akki had told him. But seconds cost gold. And if he had no sponsor and no gold, that would leave only the Stews for the dragon—and a return to bond for himself.

Jakkin stroked the bond bag once more, then buttoned his shirt over it to conceal it. He did not know yet what it felt like to be free. He had had a year of pretending in the oasis, a year of short nights and an occasional Bond-Off away from bonders' gossip and Likkarn's hard hand. But he could still endure years more as a bond boy if he had to. Balakk and Jo-Janekk had stood it well. And there would be other chances for him to steal an egg, other years. Or he could apprentice under Likkarn as a trainer, swallowing his pride and bowing and smiling like Errikkin to buy favors from the old man.

He could stand it—if he had to. But how could he give up the red to the Stews? It was not any old dragon—an enraged stud like Brother or a young cull. It was his beauty, his red. They had already shared a year together, nights and a few precious days out in the sands. He knew its mind better than his own: a deep, glowing cavern of colors and sights and sounds. He remembered the first time he had really felt his way into it, not just been assaulted by the jets and passionate lightnings it chose to send him.

He had been lying on his side, slightly winded from running. The red lay down beside him, a small mountain in the sand. Closing his eyes, Jakkin had tried to reach out for the red, and suddenly he felt it open to him and it was as if he were walking down a glowing path into a cavern where colors dripped like large, hanging crystals from a roof of the deepest purple. Rainbow puddles were on the cavern floor and multicolored fish leaped up from the water, singing. There had been a resonant thrumming, a humming that filled the air and then filled him.

The red calmed him when he was not calm, cheered him when he thought he could not be cheered. Linked as he was with it now, how could he ever bear to hear its last screams in the Stews as the sharp-bladed knack-knife cut across its tender throat links and the hot blood dripped away into the cauldrons? How could he hear that and stay sane?

Perhaps, he thought suddenly, perhaps that was why Likkarn was always yelling at the younger bonders, why he smoked blisterweed that turned his mind foggy and made him cry red tears. And perhaps that was why most dragons in the Stews were early culls or untrained yearlings. Not because they were softer, more succulent, but because no one would be linked with them to hear them when they screamed.

Jakkin's skin felt slimed with perspiration and the dragon turned and sniffed it on him. It gave out a few straggles of smoke from its slits. Jakkin fought down his own fear. If he could not control it, his red would have no chance at all. *A dragon is only as good as its master*, bonders liked to say. He took several deep breaths and then moved over to the red's head, staring into its unblinking eyes.

"Thou art a fine one, my Red," he whispered. "First fight for us both, but I trust thee." He hesitated a moment. "Trust me?"

The dragon responded with slightly rounded smokes. Deep within its eyes Jakkin thought he detected small lights.

"Dragon's fire!" he breathed. "The nearness of the other dragons must have brought it out. Thou *art* a fighter. I knew it!"

Jakkin slipped the stall ring from the red's neck and rubbed its scales underneath. They were not yet as hard as a mature fighter's—still tender enough for the knack-knife. For a moment Jakkin worried that the older Bottle O'Rum might tear the red beyond repair. He pulled the dragon's head down and whispered into its ear. "Guard thyself here," he said, rubbing with his fingers under the throat links, thinking danger at it.

The dragon shook its head playfully and Jakkin slapped it lightly on the neck, pushing it backwards and out of the stall.

The dragonlock on the wall irised open, and with a surge the red flowed through it and up into the empty Pit.

20

"It's eager." The whisper ran around the crowd. They always liked that in young dragons. Time enough to grow cautious in the Pit. Older dragons often were reluctant and had to be prodded with sticks, behind the wings or in the tender under-parts of the tail. The bettors considered it a great fault. Jakkin heard the crowd's appreciation of the red as he came up into the stands.

It would have been safer for Jakkin to remain below, guiding his dragon by mind. That way there would be no chance for Master Sarkkhan to find him.

Many trainers, Mekkle being one of them, stayed down below in the stalls drinking and eating and guiding their dragons where the sounds and look of the crowd could not influence them.

But Jakkin needed to see the red as well as feel it, to watch the fight through his own eyes as well as the red's. They had practiced too long, just the two of them, in the sands. Neither Jakkin nor his red knew how another dragon in a real fight would respond. Jakkin had to be up in the stands to understand it all. And the red was used to seeing him close by. He did not want to change that now. Not now. Besides, unlike many of the other bonders, Jakkin had never been to a fight, only read about them in the books and heard about them from Akki and his bondmates. This, he thought bitterly, might be his only chance to watch. He further rationalized that up in the stands he might find out more about Mekkle's orange, and what he learned could help him help the red.

Jakkin looked around the stands cautiously from the stairwell. He saw no one he knew, neither fellow bonders in the upper tiers nor masters who traded with Sarkkhan in the pitside seats. He edged quietly into the lower stands, just one more free boy at the fights. Nothing could call attention to him in the masters' boxes but the near-empty bond bag beneath his shirt. He checked his buttons carefully to make sure they were closed. Then he leaned forward, hands on the seatback in front of him, and watched as his red circled the ring.

It held its head high and measured the size of

the Pit, the height of the walls. It looked over the
bettors as if to count them, and an appreciative
chuckle ran through the crowd. The red scratched
in the sawdust several times, testing its depth.
And still Bottle O'Rum had not appeared.

Then with an explosion Bottle O'Rum came
through the dragonlock and landed with all four
feet planted well beneath the level of the sawdust,
his claws fastened immovably to the boards.

"Good stance," shouted someone in the crowd,
and the betting began anew.

The red gave a little flutter with its wings, a
flapping that might indicate nervousness, and Jakkin thought at it: "He is a naught. A stander. But
thy nails and wings are fresh. Do not be afraid.
Remember thy training." At that the little red's
head went high and its neck scales glittered in the
artificial sun of the pit.

"Watch that neck," shouted a heckler. "There's
one that'll be blooded soon."

"Too soon," shouted another from across the
stands at him.

Bottle O'Rum charged the inviting neck.

It was just as Jakkin hoped, for charging from
the fighting stance is a clumsy maneuver at best.
The claws must all be retracted simultaneously, or
one would catch in the boards. And the younger
the dragon the more brittle its claws. The orange
might be seven fights older than the red, but it
was not yet fully mature. As Rum charged, one of

the nails on his front right claw, probably the
unum, Jakkin thought, did catch in the floor-
boards, and it splintered, causing him to falter for
a second. The red shifted its position slightly. Instead of blooding the red on the vulnerable neck,
Rum's charge brought him headlong onto the
younger dragon's chest plates, the hardest and
slipperiest part of a fighting dragon's armor. The
screech of tooth on scale sent winces through the
crowd. Only Jakkin was ready, for it was a maneuver he had taught his dragon out in the sands.

"Now!" he cried out and thought at once.

The young red needed no urging. It bent its
neck around in a fast, vicious slash, and blood
spurted from behind the ears of Mekkle's Rum.

"First blood!" cried the crowd.

Now the betting would change, Jakkin thought
with a certain pleasure, and touched the bond bag
through the thin cloth of his shirt. Ear bites bleed
profusely but were not important. It would hurt the
orange dragon a little, like a pinprick or a splinter
does a man. It would make the dragon mad and—
more important—a bit more cautious. But first
blood! It looked good to the bettors.

Bottle O'Rum roared with the bite, loud and
piercing. It was too high up in the throat yet, but
with surprising strength. Jakkin listened carefully,
trying to judge. He had heard dragons roar at the
Nursery in anger or fear or when Likkarn had
blooded one of them for a customer intent on hear-

ing the timbre before buying. To him the roar sounded as if it had all its power in the top tones and none that resonated. Perhaps he was wrong, but if his red could make this a long fight with the orange, it might impress this crowd.

In his eagerness to help his dragon, Jakkin moved to the pit rail, elbowing his way through some older men.

"Here, boy, what do you think you're doing?" A man in a gray leather coverall spoke. He was obviously familiar with the Pits. Anyone in all-leather knew his way around. And his face, what could be seen behind the gray beard, was scored with dragonblood scars.

"Get back up in the stands. Leave ringside to the masters and money men," said his companion, taking in Jakkin's patched, food-spotted shirt and short bonder's pants with a dismissing look. He ostentatiously jounced a full bag that hung from his wrist on a leather thong; an ex-bonder often wore his old bag on his wrist.

Jakkin ignored them, fingering his badge with the facs picture of the red on it. He leaned over the rail. "Away, away good Red," he thought at his dragon and smiled when the red immediately wheeled and winged up from its blooded foe. Only then did he turn and address the two scowling bettors. "Pit right, good sirs," he said with deference, pointing at the same time to his badge.

They mumbled, but moved aside for him. A trainer, even though he had no money, had precedence at the Pit.

The orange dragon in the pit shook its head and the blood beaded its ears like a crown. A few drops spattered over the walls and into the stands. Each place a drop touched burned with that glow peculiar to the acidic dragon's blood. The onlookers ducked. One watcher in the third row of the stands was not quick enough and was seared on the cheek. He reached up a hand to the wound but did not move from his place.

The orange Rum stood up tall again and dug back into the dust.

"Another stand," said the gray-leather man to Jakkin's right.

"Pah, that's all it knows," said a dark-skinned offworlder beside him. "That's how it won its three fights. Good stance, but that's it. I wonder why I bet it at all. Let's go and get something to drink. This fight's a bore."

Jakkin watched them leave from the corner of his eye, but he absorbed their information. If the orange was a stander, if the information were true, it would help him with the fight.

The red dragon's leap back had taken it to the north side of the pit. When it saw that Bottle O'Rum had chosen to stand, it circled closer warily.

Jakkin thought at it, "He's good in the stance. Do not force him there. Make him come to thee."

The dragon's thoughts, as always, came back clearly to Jakkin, wordless but full of color and emotion. The red wanted to charge; the dragon it had blooded was waiting. The overwhelming urge was to carry the fight to the foe.

"No, my Red. Trust me. Be eager, but not foolish," cautioned Jakkin, looking for an opening.

But the crowd, as eager as the young dragon, was communicating with it, too. The yells of the men, their thoughts of charging, overpowered Jakkin's single line of calm. The red started to move.

When it saw the red bunching for a charge, Rum solidified his stance. His shoulders went rigid with the strain. Jakkin knew that if his red dived at that standing rock, it could quite easily break a small bone in its neck. And he knew from Akki's lessons in anatomy that a dragon rarely came back to the Pit once its neck bones had been re-set. Then it was good only for the breeding nurseries—if it had a fine Pit record—or the Stews.

"Steady, steady," Jakkin said, aloud. Then he shouted and waved a hand. "NO!"

The red had already started its dive, but the movement of Jakkin's hand and his shout were signals too powerful for it to ignore, and at the last possible minute it pulled to one side. As it passed, Rum slashed at it with a gaping mouth and shredded its wingtip.

"Blood," the crowd roared and waited for the red dragon to roar back.

Jakkin felt its confusion, and his head swam with the red of dragon's blood as his dragon's thoughts came to him. He watched as it soared to the top of the building and scorched its wingtip on the artificial sun, cauterizing the wound. Then, still hovering, it opened its mouth for its first blooded roar.

There was no sound.

"A mute!" called a man from the stands. He spat angrily to one side. "Never saw one before."

A wit near him shouted back, "Never heard one, either."

The crowd laughed at this, and passed the quip around the stands.

But Jakkin only stared up at his red. "A mute," he thought at it. "Oh, my poor Red. You are as powerless as I."

His use of the distancing pronoun *you* further confused the young dragon, and it began to circle downward in a disconsolate spiral, closer and closer to the waiting Rum, its mind a maelstrom of blacks and grays.

Jakkin realized his mistake in time. "It does not matter," he cried out in his mind. "Even with no roar, even voiceless, thou wilt be great." He said it with more conviction than he really felt. But it was enough for the red. It broke out of its spiral and hovered, wings working evenly.

The maneuver, however, was so unexpected that the pit-wise Bottle O'Rum was bewildered. He came out of his stance with a splattering of dust and fewmets, stopped, then charged again. The red avoided him easily, landing on his back and raking the orange scales with its claws. That drew no blood, but it frightened the older dragon into a hindfoot rise. Balancing on his tail, Rum towered nearly three meters high, his front claws scoring the air, a single shot of fire streaking from his slits.

The red backwinged away from the flames and waited.

"Steady, steady," thought Jakkin, in control again. He let his mind recall for them both the quiet sands and the cool nights when they had practiced against the reed shelter a game of charges and clawing. Then he repeated out loud, "Steady, steady."

A hard hand on his shoulder broke through his thoughts and the sweet-strong smell of blister-weed assailed him. Jakkin turned.

"Not so steady yourself," came a familiar voice.

Jakkin stared up at the ravaged face, pocked with blood scores and stained with tear-lines.

"Likkarn," breathed Jakkin, suddenly panic-stricken. He tried to turn back to the Pit, where his red waited. The hand on his shoulder was too firm, the fingers like claws through his shirt.

"And when did *you* become a dragon trainer?" the man asked.

At first Jakkin thought to bluff. The old stallboy was too sunk in his smokedreams to really listen. Bluff and run, for the wild anger that came after blisterdreams never gave a smoker time to reason. "I found . . . found an egg, Likkarn," he said. And it could be true. There were a few wild dragons, bred from escapes that had gone feral. Sometimes a lucky bonder came upon a dragon egg cache out in the sand.

The man said nothing but shook his head.

Jakkin stared at him. This was a new Likkarn—harder, full of purpose. Then Jakkin noticed. Likkarn's eyes were clearer than he had ever seen them, no longer the furious pink of the weeder, but a softer rose. Obviously he had not smoked for several days. This end of the season, Jakkin had been so intent on his own dragon that the work days at the Nursery, monitoring the mating flights, had slipped by. But Likkarn was too alert. It was useless to bluff—or to run. "I took it from the Nursery, Likkarn. I raised it in the sands. I trained it at night, by the moons."

"That's better, boy. Much better. Liars are an abomination," the man said with a bitter laugh. "And you fed it what? Goods stolen from the Master, I wager. You born-bonders know nothing. Nothing."

Jakkin's cheeks were burning now. "I am no born-bonder. My father and his father were born free. And I would never steal from the Master's stores. I planted swamp seeds in the sands last year and grew blisterweed and burnwort. And bought new seeds with my drakk bounty. *On my own time.*" He added that fiercely.

"Bonders have no time of their own," Likkarn muttered savagely. "And supplements."

"The Master says adding supplements to the food is bad for a fighter. They make a fighter fast in the beginning, but they dilute the blood." Jakkin looked into Likkarn's eyes more boldly now. "The Master said that. To a buyer." He did not add that it was Akki who had told him.

Likkarn's smile was wry and twisted. "And you eavesdrop as well." He gave Jakkin's shoulder a particularly vicious wrench.

Jakkin gasped and closed his eyes with the pain. He wanted to cry out, and thought he had, when he realized it was not his own voice he heard but a scream from the pit. He pulled away from Likkarn and stared. The scream was Bottle O'Rum's, a triumphant roar as he stood over the red whose injured wing was pinioned beneath Rum's right front claw.

"*Jakkin . . .*" came Likkarn's voice behind him, full of warning. How often Jakkin had heard that tone right before Likkarn had roused from a weed dream to the fury that always followed. Likkarn was old, but his fist was still solid.

Jakkin trembled, but he willed his focus onto the red, whose thoughts came tumbling back into his head now in a tangle of muted colors and whines. He touched his hand to the small lump under his shirt where the limp bond bag hung. He could feel his own heart beating through the leather shield. "Never mind, my Red," soothed Jakkin. "Never mind the pain. Recall the time I stood upon thy wing and we played at the Great Upset. Recall it well, thou mighty fighter. Remember. Remember."

The red stirred only slightly and made a flutter with its free wing. The crowd saw this as a gesture of submission. So did Rum, and through him, his master, Mekkle. But Jakkin did not. He knew the red had listened well and understood. The game was not over yet. Pit fighting was not all brawn; how often the books had said that. The best fighters, the ones who lasted for years, did not have to be big. They did not have to be overly strong. But they did have to be cunning gamesters, and it was this he had known about his red from the first—its love of play.

The fluttering of the unpinioned wing caught Bottle O'Rum's eye and the orange dragon turned towards it, relaxing his hold by a single nail.

The red fluttered its free wing again. Flutter

and feint. Flutter and feint. It needed the orange's attention totally on that wing. Then its tail could do the silent stalking it had learned in the sands with Jakkin.

Bottle O'Rum followed the fluttering as though laughing for his own coming triumph. His dragon jaws opened slightly in a deadly grin. If Mekkle had been in the stands instead of below in the stalls, the trick might not have worked. But the orange dragon, intent on the fluttering wing, leaned his head way back and fully opened his jaws, readying for the winning stroke. He was unaware of what was going on behind him.

"Now!" shouted Jakkin in his mind, later realizing that the entire stands had roared the words with him. Only the crowd had been roaring for the wrong dragon.

The red's tail came around with a snap, as vicious and as accurate as a driver's whip. It caught the orange on its injured ear and across an eye.

Rum screamed instead of roaring and let go of the red's wing. The red was up in an instant and leaped for Bottle O'Rum's throat.

One, two, and the ritual slashes were made. The orange throat coruscated with blood, and instantly Rum dropped to the ground.

Jakkin's dragon backed at once, slightly akilter because of the wound in its wing.

"Game to Jakkin's Red," said the disembodied voice over the speaker.

21

The crowd was strangely silent. Then a loud whoop sounded from one voice buried in the stands, a bettor who had taken a chance on the First Fighter.

That single voice seemed to rouse Bottle O'Rum. He raised his head from the ground groggily. Only his head and half his neck cleared the dust. He strained to arch his neck over, exposing the underside to the light. The two red slashes glistened like thin, hungry mouths. Then Rum began a strange, horrible humming that changed to a high-pitched whine. His body began to shake, and the shaking became part of the sound as the dust eddied around him.

The red dragon swooped down and stood before the fallen Rum, as still as stone. Then it, too, began to shake.

The sound of the orange's keening changed from a whine to a high roar. Jakkin had never heard anything like it before. He put his hands to the bond bag, then to his ears.

"What is it? What is happening?" he cried out, but the men on either side of him had moved away. Palms to ears, they backed towards the exits. Many in the crowd had already gone down the stairs, setting the thick wood walls between themselves and the noise.

Jakkin tried to reach the red dragon's mind, but all he felt were storms of orange winds, hot and blinding, and a shaft of burning white light. As he watched, the red rose up on its hind legs and raked the air frantically with its claws, as if getting ready for some last deadly blow.

"Fool's Pride," came Likkarn's defeated voice behind him, close enough to his ear to hear. "That damnable orange dragon wants death. He has been shamed, and he'll scream your red into it. Then you'll know. All you'll have left is a killer on your hands. I lost three that way. *Three.* Three dragons and three fortunes. Fool's Pride." He shouted the last at Jakkin's back, for at his first words, Jakkin had thrown himself over the railing into the pit. He landed on all fours, but was up and running at once.

He had heard of Fool's Pride, that part of the fighting dragon's bloody past that was not always bred out. Fool's Pride that led some defeated dragons to demand death. It had nearly caused the dragons to become extinct. If men had not carefully watched the lines, trained the fighters to lose with grace, there would have been no dragons left on Austar IV. He could not let his red kill. A good fighter should have a love of blooding, yes. But killing made dragons unmanageable, made them feral, made them wild. In his mind suddenly was the image of his father dying under the slashing claws of a wild orange worm. Jakkin heard a scream, thought it was an echo of his mother's voice, and realized at last it was his own.

He crashed into the red's side. "No, no," he called up at it, beating on its body with his fists. "Do not wet thy jaws in his death." He reached as high as he could and held on to the red's neck. The scales slashed his left palm cruelly, but he did not let go.

It was his touch more than his voice or his thoughts that stopped the young red. It turned slowly, sluggishly, as if rousing from a dream. Jakkin fell from its neck to the ground.

The movement shattered Bottle O'Rum's concentration. He slipped from screaming to unconsciousness in an instant.

The red nuzzled Jakkin, its eyes unfathomable, its mind still clouded. The boy stood up. Without bothering to brush the pit dust from his clothes, he thought at it, *"Thou mighty First."*

The red suddenly crowded his mind with victorious sunbursts, turned, then streaked back through the open hole to its stall and the waiting burnwort supplied by the Masters of the Pit.

As Jakkin stood there, too weary to move, Mekkle and two friends came through the stands, glowering, and leaped into the pit. They wrestled the fainting orange onto a low-wheeled cart and dragged him over to the open mecho hole by his tail. Then they shoved the beast through the hole.

Only then did Jakkin walk back to ringside, holding his cut hand palm up. It had just begun to sting.

Likkarn, still standing by the railing, was already smoking a short strand of blisterweed. He stared blankly as the red smoke circled his head.

"I owe you," Jakkin said slowly up to him, hating to admit it. "I did not know Fool's Pride when I saw it. Another minute and the red would have been good for nothing but the Stews. If I ever get a Second Fight, I will give you some of the gold. *Your bag is not yet full.*"

Jakkin meant the last phrase simply as ritual, but Likkarn's eyes suddenly roused to weed fury. His hand went to his bag. "You owe me nothing," said the old man. He held his head high and the age lines on his neck crisscrossed like old fight scars. "*Nothing.* You owe the Master everything. I need no reminder that I am a bonder. A boy. *I fill my bag myself.*"

Jakkin bowed his head under the old man's assault. "Let me tend the red's wounds. Then do with me as you will." He bowed and, without waiting for an answer, ducked through the mecho hole and slid down the shaft.

Jakkin came to the stall where the red was already at work grooming itself, polishing its scales with a combination of fire and spit. He slipped the ring around its neck and knelt down by its side. Briskly he put his hand out to touch its wounded wing, in a hurry to finish the examination before Likkarn came down. The red drew back at his touch, sending into his mind a mauve landscape dripping with gray tears.

"Hush, little flametongue," crooned Jakkin, using the lullaby sounds he had invented to soothe the hatchling of the sands. "I won't hurt thee. I want to help."

But the red continued to retreat from him, crouching against the wall.

Puzzled, Jakkin pulled his hand back. Yet still the red huddled away, and a spurt of yellow-red fire flamed from its slits. "Not here, furnace-lung," said Jakkin, annoyed. "That will set the stall on fire."

A rough hand pushed him aside. It was Likkarn, no longer in the weed dream but starting into the uncontrollable fury that capped a weed

223

sequence. The dragon, its mind wide open with the pain of its wound and the finish of the fight, had picked up Likkarn's growing anger and reacted to it.

"You don't know wounds, boy," growled Likkarn. "How could you? I'll show you what a *real* trainer knows." He grabbed the dragon's torn wing and held it firmly, then with a quick motion, and before Jakkin could stop him, he set his mouth on the jagged tear.

The dragon reared back in alarm and pain and tried to whip its tail around, but the stalls were purposely built small to curb such motion. Its tail scraped along the wall and barely tapped the man. Jakkin grabbed at Likkarn's arm with both hands and furiously tore him from the red's wing.

"I'll kill you, you weeder," he screamed. "Can't you wait till a dragon is in the Stews before you try to eat it? I'll kill you." He slammed at Likkarn with his fist and feet, knowing as he did it that the man's weed anger would be turned on him and he might be killed by it, and not caring.

Suddenly Jakkin felt himself being lifted up from behind, his legs dangling, kicking uselessly at the air. A man's strong arm around his waist held him fast. At the same time, the man pushed Likkarn back against the wall.

"Hold off, boy. Hold off. He was a good trainer —once."

22

Jakkin twisted around as best he could and saw the man he had most feared seeing. It was Master Sarkkhan himself, dressed in a leather suit of the red and gold Nursery colors. His red beard was brushed out, making it twice as bushy as normal. He looked grim.

"Hold off," Sarkkhan said again. "And hear me. Likkarn is right about the best way to deal with a wing wound. An open tear, filled with dragon's blood, will burn the tongue surely. But a man's tongue heals quickly, and there is something in human saliva that closes these small rips."

Sarkkhan put Jakkin down but held onto his shoulder with one large hand.

"It's the other way round, too," Jakkin heard

his voice saying in a rush. "The dragon licked my wound and it healed clean."

"Well, now, that I never saw myself, though it's been folk wisdom around here for a while." Sarkkhan brushed his hair back from a forehead that was pitted with blood scores as evenly spaced as a bonder's chain. "Now, promise me you will let this old man look to the red's wing."

"I will not," Jakkin said hotly. "He's a weeder and he's as likely to rip the wing as heal it. And the red hates him—just as I do." Suddenly realizing who he was talking to, Jakkin put his hand up before his mouth.

Likkarn turned towards him and raised a fist, aiming it at Jakkin's head. Before it could land, the dragon had pulled the ring chain free of the stall and nosed the trainer to the ground, putting a front foot on him to hold him still.

Master Sarkkhan let go of Jakkin's shoulder and considered the red for a moment. "Likkarn," he said at last, nodding his head at the old man, "I think the boy is right. The dragon won't have you. It's too closely linked. I had wondered at that, by its actions in the pit. This confirms it. Wish I knew how he did it. That close a linkage is rare. I can control my dragons somewhat. But a fresh dragon and a trainer are never that close. It takes years to establish such a bond. Never mind now. Best leave this to the boy and me."

Jakkin nodded, saying, "Let him go, my worm."
At his words, the dragon lifted its foot slowly.

Likkarn got up clumsily and brushed off his
clothes. One button of his shirt had been ripped off
and the bond bag had slipped out in the scuffle.
Jakkin was surprised to see that it was more than
halfway plump, jangling with coins. How could
he have filled his bag that way in less than a year?
Betting? Perhaps he hadn't spent his Bond-Offs
weeding, but playing the dragons at Krakkow Pit.

Likkarn caught Jakkin's look and angrily stuffed
that bag back inside his shirt, then jabbed at the
outline of Jakkin's thin bag with a weed-reddened
finger. "And how much have *you* got there? Not
even a baby's portion, I warrant." He walked off
with as much dignity as he could muster, then
slumped by the stairwell to watch.

Sarkkhan, ignoring them both, was crouching
down by the dragon, letting it get the smell of
him. He caressed its jaws and under its neck with
his large, scarred hands. Slowly the big man
worked his way back towards the wings, crooning
at the dragon in low tones, smoothing its scales,
all the while staring into its eyes. Slowly the
membranes, top and bottom, shuttered the red's
eyes, and it relaxed. Only then did Sarkkhan let
his hand close over the wounded wing. The
dragon gave a small shudder but was otherwise
quite still.

"Your red did a good job searing its wound on the light. Did you teach it that?"

"No," the boy admitted.

"Of course not. Foolish of me. How could you? No lamps in the sands. Good breeding, then," said Sarkkhan with a small chuckle of appreciation. "And I should know. After all, your dragon's mother is my best—Heart O'Mine."

"You . . . you knew all along then." Jakkin suddenly felt as confused as a blooded First.

Sarkkhan stood up and stretched. In the confines of the stall he seemed enormous, a red-gold giant. Jakkin suddenly felt smaller than his fourteen years.

"*Fewmets*, boy, of course I knew," Sarkkhan answered. "Even when I'm not around, I know *everything* that happens at my nursery. Everything. Make it my business to know."

Jakkin collapsed down next to his dragon and put his arm over its neck. Akki. It had to have been Akki, because who but Akki had known everything about him. She had sold him to Sarkkhan and this was the price he had to pay: the knowledge that all of his manhood was the gift of the girl with the mocking mouth and her red-bearded lover. What had she said? "I have kept my promise in substance—if not in words." And she lied then, too. He had believed each one of her lies, believed them because he wanted to, because it was dark-haired Akki who told them. Well, he would not think about it any longer. It was too shameful, too painful.

When Jakkin finally spoke again, it was in a very small voice. "Then why did you let me do it? Were you trying to get me in trouble? Do you want me in jail? Or did you just find it all terribly funny, your own private entertainment?"

The man threw back his head and roared, and the dragons in neighboring stalls stirred uneasily at the sound. Even Likkarn started at the laugh and a trainer six stalls down growled in disapproval. Sarkkhan looked down at the boy. "I'm sorry, boy, I keep forgetting how young you are. Never known anyone quite that young to train a hatchling successfully. But everyone gets a chance to steal one egg. It's a kind of test, you might say. The only way to break out of bond. Some are meant to be bonders, some masters. How else can you tell which is which? Likkarn's tried it—endless times—but he just can't make it, eh, old boy?" The master glanced over at Likkarn with a look akin to affection, but Likkarn only glared back. "Steal an egg and try. The only things wrong to steal are a bad egg or your master's provisions." Sarkkhan stopped talking for a minute and mused. Idly he ran a hand over the red dragon's back as it chewed contentedly on its burnwort, little gray straggles of smoke easing from its slits. "Of course most *do* steal bad eggs or are too impatient to train what comes out, and instead they make a quick sale to the Stews just for a few coins to jangle in their bags. Then it's back to bond again before a month is out."

Jakkin interrupted. "I didn't steal an egg, sir."

"I know, boy. I always had high hopes for you. You kept yourself apart from the others. Had a kind of *dedication* about you. A dream you wouldn't dilute with cheap, boyish pleasures. Your coins went into your own bag, not into someone else's. You filled your bag yourself. I like that. I admire that. So I left one late hatcher uncounted, just in case. I knew you could read—and count. I had high hopes and you didn't let me down, even though you lay a week in the hospice. And didn't I give Likkarn a de-bagging for that, for killing Brother and nearly killing you. And you bounced back. Stole a hatchling from my best hen. Probably the best hatchling in the bunch. None of that false compassion—picking a runt or one with an injured wing. You went right to the best. I like that. I'd do it myself."

Jakkin started to say something, but Sarkkhan went on.

"That's all you stole, I hope. The ones who steal provisions land in jail. And the next time, it's off-planet for good."

"You wouldn't put me in jail, then? Or the red in the Stews? I couldn't let you do that, Master Sarkkhan. Not even you," Jakkin said.

"Send a First Fighter, a *winner,* to the Stews? *Fewmets,* boy. Where's your brain? Been smoking blisterweed?" Sarkkhan hunkered down next to him.

Jakkin looked down at his sandals; his feet were soiled from the dust of the pit. He ordered his stomach to calm down and felt an answering muted rainbow of calm from the dragon. Then a sudden, peculiar thought came to him.

"Did you have to steal an egg, Master Sarkkhan? Or were you born free?"

The big redheaded man laughed again and thrust his right hand into Jakkin's face. Jakkin drew back, but Sarkkhan was holding up two fingers and waggling them before his eyes.

"Two! I stole two. A male and a female. Blood Type and Heart's Ease. And it was not mere chance. Even then I knew the difference. *In the egg.* I knew. I can tell in the egg, and by a hatchling. Even before the first mating season exposes the difference. And *that's* why I'm the best breeder on Austar IV." He stood up abruptly and held out his hand to the boy. "But enough. The red is fine and you are due upstairs." He yanked Jakkin to his feet and seemed at once to lose his friendliness.

"Upstairs?" Jakkin could not think what that meant. "You said I was not to go to jail. I want to stay with the red. I want . . ."

"*Wormwort*, boy, have you been listening or not? You have to register that dragon. Give her a name. Record her as a First Fighter, a winner."

"Her?" Jakkin heard only the one word.

"Yes, a her. Do you challenge *me* on that? Me? And I want to come with you and collect my gold. I bet a bagful on that red of yours—on Likkarn's advice. He's been watching you train, my orders. He said she was looking good, and *sometimes* I believe him."

Jakkin pulled his hand back. "Likkarn? Likkarn watched? But it was Akki. It had to be. Her footprints. Akki who told . . ." He trailed off into a confused silence.

Sarkkhan shook his head. "That little piece of baggage. Just like her mother, boy. But when she's a woman, she'll be something, I'll tell you. Oh, I knew she'd been sneaking out there to be with you. As I said, there's not much I don't know about my Nursery. And when I first heard about it from Likkarn, about you staying out half the night making love to my girl . . ."

Jakkin started to protest, but Master Sarkkhan's voice overrode his. "Well, you can bet I was ready to kick your tail up between your shoulderblades till your bondshirt rattled up your backbone like a window shade. I'm not an easy father, I'm not."

"Father!"

"And her refusing to let me claim her officially, to write it into the books. Akkhina out of Rakki by

Sarkkhan James. I'm not supposed to let anyone know. She's got a temper, that one. Just like her father." He laughed. "Won't have anything to do with me. Me! The best breeder on the planet. Pretending to be a bonder and wearing that damned foolish empty bag after I bought off her bond. Fool's Pride, I shouldn't wonder. Damnably silly. There are masters and there are bonders in this world and no one *wants* to be a bonder. 'Let her try to fill her bag alone,' Likkarn said. 'Then she'll come crawling back,' he said. And *sometimes* I listen to him. Sometimes. I owe him still. He took me in, taught me everything."

The day seemed made up of never-ending surprises. Jakkin kept hearing himself repeat Sarkkhan's last words like a Common Mocker, the little lizard that mimicked the tail-end of its enemy's challenges and, in the ensuing confusion, often got away. Only Jakkin could not tear himself away from Sarkkhan's endless stream of revelations. "You owe him? Likkarn? *He* taught *you*?"

"*Fewmets*, boy, you sound like a Mocker. Yes, I owe him. He found me, a runaway bond boy, out in the sand near Rokk with two eggs. Trying to hatch them with my own body warmth. Damn near froze to death in Dark-After. He found me and dragged me to a shelter and warmed me with his own clothes. Didn't turn me in either, though it could have bought him out of bond. Took three of my hatchlings in exchange when the two mated,

233

and that's the first time he was a master. I owe him." Sarkkhan walked towards the stairwell where the old trainer still waited.

They stopped by Likkarn, who was slumped again in another blisterweed dream. Sarkkhan reached out and took the stringy red weed ash from the old man's hand. He threw it on the floor and ground it savagely into the dust. "He wasn't born a weeder, boy. And he hasn't forgotten all he once knew. But he'll never be a *real* man. Hasn't got the guts to stay out of bond. I hope you do." Then, shaking his head, Master Sarkkhan moved up the stairs, impatiently waving a hand at the boy to follow.

A stray strand of color-pearls passed through Jakkin's mind and he turned around to look at the dragon's stall. Then he gulped and said in a rush at Sarkkhan's back, "But she's a mute, Master Sarkkhan. She may have won this fight by wiles, but she's a mute. No one will bet on a dragon that cannot roar."

The man reached down and grabbed Jakkin's hand, yanking him through the doorway and up the stairs. They mounted two at a time. "You really are lizard waste," said Sarkkhan, punctuating his sentences with another step. "Why do you think I sent a half-blind weeder skulking around the sands at night watching you train a snatchling and make love to my girl? Because I'd lost my mind? *Fewmets*, boy. Likkarn was the only bonder I could trust to keep his mouth shut. And I need to know what is happening to every damned dragon I have bred. I have had a hunch and a hope these past twenty-five years, breeding small-voiced dragons together. I've been *trying* to breed a mute. Think of it, a mute fighter—why, it would give nothing away, not to pit foes or to bettors. A mute fighter and its trainer . . ." and Sarkkhan stopped on the stairs, looking down at the boy. "Why, they'd rule the Pits, boy."

They finished the stairs and turned down the hallway. Sarkkhan strode ahead and Jakkin had to doubletime in order to keep up with the big man's strides.

"Master Sarkkhan," he began at the man's back.

Sarkkhan did not break stride but growled, "I'm no longer your master, Jakkin. *You* are a master now. A master trainer. That dragon will speak only to you, go only on your command. Remember that and act accordingly. Never have seen such a linkage as you have with that worm. It's a wonder, it is. If I was a jealous man . . . but I'm not."

Jakkin blinked twice and touched his chest. "But . . . but my bag is empty. I have no gold to fill it. I have no sponsor for my next fight. I . . ."

Sarkkhan whirled, and his eyes were fierce. "*I* am sponsor for your next fight. I thought that much, at least, was clear. And when your bag is full, you will pay me no gold for your bond. Instead I want pick of the first hatching when the red is bred—to a mate of my choosing. If she is a complete mute, she may breed true, and *I* mean to have that hatchling."

"Oh, Master Sarkkhan," Jakkin cried, suddenly realizing that all his dreams were realities, that there was no price to pay at all, "you may have the pick of the first *three* hatchings." He grabbed the man's hand and tried to shake his thanks into it.

"*Fewmets!*" the man yelled, startling some of the passers-by. He shook the boy's hand loose. "How can you ever become a bettor if you offer it all up front. You have to disguise your feelings better than that. Offer me the pick of the *third* hatching. Counter me. Make me work for whatever I get."

Jakkin said softly, testing, "The pick of the third."

"First two," said Sarkkhan, softly back, and his smile came slowly. Then he roared, "Or I'll have you in jail and the red in the Stews."

A crowd began to gather around them, betting on the outcome of the uneven match. Sarkkhan was a popular figure at pit fights and the boy was leather-patched, obviously a bonder, an unknown, worm waste.

All at once Jakkin felt as if he were at pitside. He felt the red's mind flooding into his, a rainbow effect that gave him a rush of courage. It was a game, then, all a game. Being a master, being a man, just meant learning the rules and how far to go. And he knew how to play. "The second," said Jakkin, smiling back. "After all, Heart's Blood is a First Fighter, and a winner. And," he hissed at Sarkkhan so that only the two of them could hear, "she's a mute." Then he stood straight and said loudly so that it carried to the crowd. "You'll be lucky to have pick of the second."

Sarkkhan stood silently as if considering both the boy and the crowd. He brushed his hair back from his forehead, exposing the blood scores, nodded. "Done," he said. "A hard bargain." Then he reached over and ruffled Jakkin's hair, saying back, "And I'll be glad to give my girl Akki to you. She needs a strong master." They walked off together.

The crowd, settling their bets, let them through.

"I *thought* you were a good learner," Sarkkhan said to the boy. "Second it is. Though," and he chuckled quietly, "you should remember this. There is rarely anything very good in a first hatching. That is something Likkarn has never learned. Second is the best by far."

"I didn't know that," said Jakkin.

"Why should you?" countered Sarkkhan. "*You* are not the best breeder on Austar IV. I am. But I like the name you picked. Heart's Blood out of Heart O'Mine. It suits."

They went through the doorway together to register the red and to stuff Jakkin's bag with his hard-earned dragon's gold.

23

The twin moons cast shadows like blood scores across the sand. Jakkin hunkered down in the bowl-shaped depression and listened. Inside the wood-and-stone Dragonry he could hear the mewling and scratching of hatchlings as they pipped out of their shells. One more night, maybe two, and the hatching would be complete.

Near the stud barn was a newer, smaller barn. In that building Heart's Blood stayed apart from the other hens. She was still too young to breed, though under Sarkkhan's tutelage she and Jakkin had won two more fights. Sarkkhan said that Heart's Blood would command the best mating prices if she fought at least ten times in a variety of minor pits. After that, if she could win a championship in a Major Pit, she would be known all over the world.

"Sleep, my worm," Jakkin thought as he stood and walked past the barn. A cool river of greens meandered slowly through his mind in response. He knew that Likkarn was asleep in the bond-house and no other watchers had been set on his track. Sarkkhan trusted him. He would not betray that trust. Brooming his footsteps away for the first kilometer would not keep Likkarn or Sark-khan from his private spot, but it would keep the other bonders from finding it. He still needed a place he could go. And he hoped that Akki might be waiting for him there.

He remembered the first time he had gone back, several weeks after the fight with Rum. Wanting to claim the remaining rows of weed and wort plants in order to keep his debt to Sarkkhan down, he stripped the stalks with care. He had been at work for only a few minutes when he heard a fa-miliar mocking laugh. He turned and had seen Akki standing near the shelter, her hands on her hips.

"I hear you won," she said. "Ardru was there. In the Master Box. Did you see him? Was it exciting? Was it worth the risk?"

He had walked over to her slowly. "Why haven't you returned to the Nursery?" he asked.

"Do you always answer questions with a ques-tion?" she countered. They had both laughed.

Later she told him she would never come back. "I only stayed as long as I did to help you. Because you had a dream, just like me. If dreamers don't help one another . . . But once *your* dream came true, it was time for me to go. I don't really belong in a Nursery. Not anymore. I am both master and bonder," she said. "And I will let no man fill my bag."

Then she added, almost under her breath, "I left the gold Sarkkhan paid for my bond on his pillow."

Jakkin did not ask her how she got the gold.

"I know Sarkkhan is your father," he said quietly.

"I am not responsible for that."

"Then why must you go away?" he asked.

"I just told you," she said. "Weren't you listening?"

"You answered my question with a question," Jakkin whispered. "I don't want you to go."

She said nothing, just looked at him strangely, and left.

The second time she had come during the day when Jakkin had taken Heart's Blood for a run and a day of training. The dragon was often restless if he left her confined too long in the barn. She needed to fly in great wheeling arcs over the oasis. And Jakkin always felt he had passed some kind of important test each time the dragon returned to his side.

It was Heart's Blood who had first sensed Akki's approach, casting a gold silhouette in Jakkin's mind. He recognized it immediately as Akki, though it was many minutes more before she actually came into view.

"How do you know when I am going to be here?" he asked.

"I don't. Sometimes I come when you aren't here," she said. "And I lie down by the pool and remember. Or forget."

He wanted to ask, "Remember what? Forget what?" But he didn't. Instead, he lay down in the sand with his head resting on the dragon's flank. Akki sat beside him. They held hands. That was the day they hardly spoke at all.

The last time he had seen Akki was a night when he had come out to the oasis to sit and think and be by himself. He had been worrying about an approaching fight and his nervousness had communicated itself to Heart's Blood. So he had come alone, expecting no one.

It had been a night of many breezes, and the swirling patterns of sand had changed over and over, a kaleidoscope whose pieces were shaken by the winds.

Jakkin had been sitting by the shelter with his

eyes closed when suddenly he felt Akki by his side. She had moved up close to him without warning, putting her hands on either side of his face. Her palms felt as hot as dragon's blood on his cheeks.

She pulled him towards her and kissed him slowly, gently. She seemed to know what she was doing and he let himself almost drown in the sweetness of her kiss. Then she pulled away suddenly and said, "I have to go away. *Really* go away this time."

He had laughed nervously, saying, "You can't, you know. You belong here. With me. Your father gave you to me. He said you needed a master."

She stood up. "You're such a boy, sometimes, Jakkin Stewart. Such a child. And so is he." She turned and walked away.

Jakkin had scrambled up after her, but she had run from him across the sand. He tried to follow her and suddenly heard the roar of a truck engine ahead of him. All he found were deep tire ruts in the sand.

Jakkin came upon the oasis and listened, stroking the bond bag he still wore around his neck. It was plump and jangling with coins. He had earned enough from the three fights to pay Sarkkhan his bond and to buy Errikkin's bondpaper as well. He still owed Sarkkhan: gold for the barn and for feed, and the choice of the second hatching.

But he owed it freely, master to master. He was his own master now. He need not wear his bag.

But Jakkin had sworn to himself that he would wear it until he could pour out the gold from the bag into Akki's hands and she accepted him as a master and a man. It was a promise he made to himself, and he was a man who kept his promises. He hoped he would not have to wait too long.